Praise for
The Captain and the Girl

"Knock-out book...his writing is simple, yet smart, and he's a natural storyteller." – Mark Dwyer, *The Newfoundland Herald*

"Pilgrim skillfully builds up his story to a grisly and gripping climax." – Roberta Buchanan, *The Downhomer*

"Earl Pilgrim has a tendency to jump into things and come out a winner, whether it be writing, protecting wildlife or sparring in the boxing ring." – Glen Whiffen, *The Telegram*

"[Pilgrim is] a born storyteller...the same impact he has when talking face to face translates onto the page." – Craig Welsh, *The Express*

"A natural-born storyteller, Earl B. Pilgrim will not disappoint his fans with...*The Captain and the Girl*. It will forever resonate through my psyche. I thank Pilgrim for telling a story which had to be told." – Karen Shewbridge, *The Telegram*

The Captain

AND THE GIRL

The Captain

AND THE GIRL

Earl B. Pilgrim

Flanker Press Ltd.
St. John's, Newfoundland
2001

Library and Archives Canada Cataloguing in Publication

Pilgrim, Earl B. (Earl Baxter), 1939-
    The captain and the girl

ISBN 1-894463-18-8

1. Title.

PS8587.I338C36 2001	C813'.54	C2001-902706-0
PR9199.3.P493C36 2001		

PRINTED IN CANADA

FLANKER PRESS
ST. JOHN'S, NL, CANADA
TOLL FREE: 1-866-739-4420
WWW.FLANKERPRESS.COM

COVER ART: ADAM FREAKE

First Canadian edition printed September 2001

10 9 8 7 6 5 4

We acknowledge the financial support of: the Government of Canada through the Book Publishing Industry Development Program (BPIDP); the Canada Council for the Arts which last year invested $20.3 million in writing and publishing throughout Canada; the Government of Newfoundland and Labrador, Department of Tourism, Culture and Recreation.

- Acknowledgements -

I wish to thank the following people who contributed in many ways to the research and writing of this book:

Special thanks to my wife Beatrice, Baine and Nancy Pilgrim, Ceasar and Barbara Pilgrim, Norman and Marsha Pilgrim, and Nadine Ellsworth.

In Roddickton, Bob Ropson, Clifford and Emma Brown, and the historian of Conche, Mr. Paddy O'Neill.

Gid and Alma Tucker of Lewisporte.

In Labrador City, Les Budden, Ivan and Ramona Manuel, and Junior Canning.

Gary Newell of the Sir Wilfred Thomason Grenfell Historical Society, Paul Canning of the International Grenfell Association, and Austin Canning.

John Goodyear, Roddickton, and Mrs. Dorothy Goodyear of Grand Falls.

Thanks to Erin Riche of St. John's, model for the cover.

And Vera McDonald and Margo Cranford of St. John's, and Greta (Lear) Hussey of Port de Grave.

Note: The names of some of the people in this book have been changed to protect their privacy.

Dedicated to my grandmother, Emily Jane (Crane) Roberts, of Brandy Harbour (now Cooks Harbour).

Grandmother Roberts was fifteen years old when her father offered her to a skipper on his way to fish on the Labrador. She never returned home, and she never saw her father again.

Foreword

I once heard the great Little Jimmy Dickens sing and narrate a song, and it went something like this:

> In the world's mighty gallery of pictures,
> There hangs the scenes that are painted from life,
> There are pictures of youth and of beauty,
> And there are pictures of peace and of strife,
> There are pictures of love and of passion,
> Of old age and of blushing young brides,
> But the saddest of all that hangs on the wall,
> Is the picture of life's other side.

If the scenes along the Labrador coast and the Great Northern Peninsula of Newfoundland could have been captured on film or audio tape or on a canvas hanging on the wall, especially around the time when Sir Wilfred Grenfell, M.D. arrived to carry out his medical mission of mercy, they would be something to behold.

As I began this story, my thoughts pulled back the covers of the old stories that were told to me in the 1950s by my dear old grandmother, Emily Jane Roberts. She came from a little town called Brandy Harbour, later renamed Cooks Harbour, which is located at the top of the Great Northern Peninsula. In her early days—she was born in the 1880s—when the rough and daring fishing skippers were prosecuting the cod-fishery on the Labrador coast, they would search frantically for a female cook to take with them as they went north. Sometimes they took young girls without anyone's permission, but in most cases the families in these outports were so poor they gladly gave their daughters to those crews if they were guaranteed safe passage and food for the summer.

Some were as young as twelve years old, and most weren't paid. Grandmother Roberts was fifteen when she was offered to one of these fishing skippers on his way to the Labrador. Captain Peter Brooks, a small fish merchant out of Lushes Bight, had run into a heavy storm and was driven into Cooks Harbour, and Emily Jane's father thought he was a wonderful good man, so he packed her meagre bags and shipped her off with this old skipper and his crew to Labrador.

Before Grandmother Roberts got aboard the boat to go out to the schooner, she stood on the beach and looked back at her father. Her mother had died giving birth to her, and he was her last remaining relative. William Crane stood there with tears running down his face, and he put his arms around her and kissed her, saying, "Emily, my dear, I love you, and I want you to promise me that if we never meet again on earth, we'll meet again in heaven."

With these words he turned and walked away without looking back. It was the last time they ever saw each other.

Grandmother Roberts was one of many young women who were either given up or forced to live with fishing crews on the coasts of Newfoundland and Labrador. She eventually married my grandfather, Azariah Roberts, and spent a long and happy life serving in the Salvation Army.

But many of those girls were not so lucky.

Here now is the story of how Dr. Wilfred Grenfell arrived by boat on the Labrador coast in 1892 and was storm-driven into a little cove nestled between two islands. I invite you to come along with me and walk in the footsteps of this great pioneer and peek into a medical file called THE CAPTAIN AND THE GIRL.

PART I

ON THE LABRADOR

Newfoundland
and Labrador

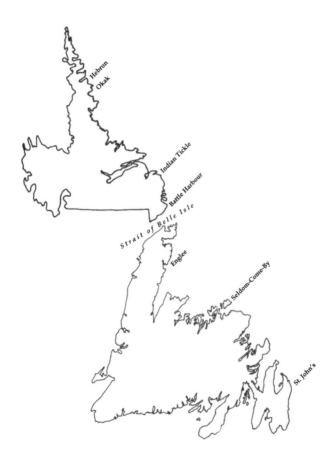

Hebron
Okak
Indian Tickle
Battle Harbour
Strait of Belle Isle
Englee
Seldom-Come-By
St. John's

ONE

The little schooner rolled on its side as the seven men winched the trap punt aboard. The swell was a sure sign that it would be a rough day on the ocean outside the shelter of the harbour. Skipper Joe Budden wasn't worried, because the swells came from rough seas created by strong winds off-shore, which he welcomed to fill the sails and push his schooner down to the Labrador.

This was the year 1892, a time when canvas was the only means by which fishermen from the colony of Newfoundland and Labrador could power their fishing schooners. Steam was fast becoming a reality, but wind was the only means affordable for the majority of those who pulled fish from the ocean.

Skipper Joe was one of these. He was classed as one who was a good fishermen, and he could sail and navigate the northeast coast of the island and the coast of Labrador without a chart or compass most of the time. He was a dependable man who spent all his life going north.

Skipper Joe Budden came from a family of fifteen children. His father before him was a fisherman who had spent most of his life doing the very same thing his son Joe did, but the younger Budden was a different man in his ways. He had been a very religious person for most of his life, following in the footsteps of his mother.

On board Skipper Joe's schooner were his supplies for the long summer months, enough to outfit his crew until the last of September. He had just left the merchant's wharf, where he had taken on a full load of salt, the most important item in his cargo, for without it there would be no fishing. Salt was the only means of curing fish in large bulk during this period of Newfoundland's history, and this was usually a full schooner-load if the fishing was good. Other items included twine and iron grapnels, cod traps, salmon nets, trawls and handline jiggers. Boat-repair material was also stacked on deck, along with firewood for the summer, and a large pile of lumber that would be used to construct a small shack and a place where they could process their fish onshore.

The main food supplies were flour, salt pork, salt beef, hard bread and molasses. Some tea was taken aboard, but no sugar or milk, since they weren't considered part of a fisherman's everyday diet, and the fish merchants kept it off the inventory of supplies. Sugar was substituted with molasses, because it was easy to transport and adaptable to many recipes.

Stacked below deck were rolls of canvas to be used for mending the sails. In an emergency, they could be shaped into a pair of rough pants or shirts. Cooking and the mending of the fishermen's meagre homemade clothes were done by the men themselves if there was no girl or woman aboard, and this would be done by lamplight, after a hard day's work.

It was late May, and the weather was warm and sunny after a cool, late spring. The rough ice had all but moved off from the coast, and the leftovers were large bergs that decorated the shoreline. Standing tall and gleaming in the sunlight like headstones in a graveyard, they were grim reminders of doom for those who dared enter their chilled waters.

Two weeks before Skipper Joe set out for the Labrador, he hinted to his four sons that it would be of great benefit to the crew if a cook went with them this summer. It would be next to impossible to have a man accompany them as a cook, because they would have to give him a share of the catch.

He could follow the lead of most other merchants who provided no pay, just food and lodging, but that wasn't Skipper Joe's way of operating. If he found someone, he would pay five dollars per month in addition to the usual benefits, and with that kind of an incentive he received offers from half a dozen young girls and older women. He had the pick of whomever he wanted, and as he went down through the list of names, there was one girl, Molly, who kept coming to the top as the number one candidate. He called a meeting with his four sons and the two other crewmen going, and he put forward her name.

"What do you think of her, men?" he asked. "Do you think she would be a wise choice?"

They all agreed that she would be best, because they knew her well.

Molly was a beautiful eighteen-year-old girl, tall, with dark hair and blue eyes. She came from a very quiet family, her father a fisherman who stayed at home and fished the ocean near the small settlement, and her mother a hard worker who helped cure the fish, grow vegetables in the garden, and make hay for the goats and sheep. Young Molly was no stranger to hard work; the gene of responsibility was bred in her.

On May 28, 1892, she stood on the deck of the rolling schooner. She looked back at her home and at her mother and family, who were waving to her.

Molly waved back. "Goodbye, Mother."

She knew her mother hadn't heard her. The blocks in the rigging were screeching to the pull of ropes as the men hauled up the fluttering sails in the southwest wind that gave the boat momentum as it slowly moved away from the dockside houses and out the harbour.

"Have you ever been out in a schooner, Molly?" asked the skipper.

"No, sir, I haven't, but I've been out in a trap boat many times with my father."

"Well, that's good. You should make a good sailor."

"I hope so, sir," she said.

Skipper Joe looked at the sky over Molly's shoulder. "If the wind stays like this all day, by the time dark overtakes us we should be at Horse Island."

Molly nodded, but knew nothing of what he was saying; all she knew was that she was going to cook on the Labrador and that she was on her way.

It is a known and documented fact that the life of a fisherman travelling to the Labrador back in the days of sails and wooden schooners was a dismal and rugged one, but the fight to exist in those days made every man and woman grin and bear it. If they didn't, their chances of survival were slim. Many a story has been told about men, women and children becoming shipwrecked on the way to their favourite fishing grounds down north, going adrift on the cold, briny ocean, dying and disappearing in the depths of a watery grave where their bones would be picked clean by bottom scavengers. Some actually made Labrador, only to die lonely deaths from disease or injury, far away from medical help and the comfort of family.

The small schooner lay at anchor in one of the harbours along the Great Northern Peninsula. A swell was rolling, and the creaking of wood sometimes went silent as the men sat in the glow of their cod-oil torches, their faces made to look a deep orange colour. The dim, flickering flames made their shadows jump as they sat around the forecastle table after supper. There they sat, spinning yarns of tokens and fairies and the ghosts of people long dead.

Skipper Joe sat near the stove and was keeping the fire going after Molly had filled the oven with bread. The smell of the baking bread combined with the pungent odour of the torches to create a peculiar blend that lulled the men at the table to the brink of sleep.

The skipper stirred and looked at his pocket watch. "Molly," he called, "your bread should be ready to take out of the oven, my dear."

Molly was lying in her bunk, staring at the dancing shadows on the planking overhead. Her face was clearly visible to the old skipper. Her hair was jet black, with eyelashes to match, and her deep blue eyes made her look all the more attractive. She was well built and a little above average height. He thought she was the most beautiful girl he had ever seen.

She saw the skipper move toward the oven. "Did you call for me, Skipper?" she asked.

"Yes, I was wondering about the bread, my dear. I think it should be ready by now. But that's all right. Stay where you are; I'll check it."

"Oh, my," she said as she jumped up. "I'll do it, Skipper." She quickly moved to the stove and opened the oven door. "Yes, it's done, sir. Thank you for reminding me. I got carried away with the story Bill was telling."

"That's all right. Put the rest in the oven and I'll watch it. You can lie down if you want, now that the stories are over."

"No, sir, but thanks. I'm not tired."

"I noticed just now that you were doing a lot of thinking," said Skipper Joe.

"Yes, I was."

"Are you sorry for coming with us, Molly?"

"Why, no, sir. I'm glad to be along. I think we'll have a wonderful summer together down on the Labrador."

"If we all pull together and work hard, we'll overcome any kind of problems that we run into. If we do that, we'll have a good trip."

"Yes, sir." Molly finished putting the pans of risen dough in the oven and went back to her bunk.

The forecastle in the schooner usually accommodated a group of rough-and-tumble men, designed in such a way that it was a combined sleeping quarters and kitchen and dining room area. The bunks were about four feet apart near the floor, and six feet apart at the top. Between the bunks, in the aisle, was a table with a stool along each side. Molly's bed was a bottom bunk at the front of the forecastle, where the men had put up a screen so that whenever she went to bed she could pull it across for privacy.

On board his vessel, Skipper Joe Budden operated with a firm hand, with clear rules of work, and no foolishness or laziness tolerated. The men knew what to expect for the next two to three months, what was permissible and what was forbidden. They were going to the Labrador to fish for cod and for nothing else, and each was willing to sacrifice the conveniences of home for however long it took to fill the hold with salted cod. Disagreements were not tolerated, all orders were obeyed with respect, and everyone slept the sleep of an honest toiler.

Skipper Joe had four sons, and they had all come with him on this particular trip. The oldest was Bill, thirty-four, and the youngest, Jack, was eighteen, the same age as Molly. Roy and Fred were his two other sons, hard-working and loyal, and the extra crewmen accompanying Skipper Joe and his sons were Hap and Gid, two dependable men they had signed on. This was Jack's fifth year going to the Labrador. He was now a grown man, tall and strong, and with his blazing red hair and freckles he stood apart from his brothers.

In those days of sail and slave labour, it was a custom that as long as a man stayed single he would give his parents half his earnings until he reached the age of twenty-one. Around the outports cash didn't exist, and for this reason Jack gave his father all that he made with no questions asked. The five dollars per month that Molly earned would have to be taken up in goods at the store of the fish merchant who supplied them for their voyage.

Tonight, Molly was too excited to sleep, being young and going away from home for such a long time. She wanted to talk to Jack, but she also knew that it would be dangerous to do so. She had strict orders, not only from the skipper but also from her mother, not to be caught alone with a man after dark.

Opposite Molly's bunk, just four feet away, Jack leaned up on his elbow. He watched with great curiosity as Molly pulled the screen across and went about getting ready for bed. He could see the bottoms of her feet in the dim, flickering light as she knelt down to say her prayers, and by the light of the little candle she had perched high on a shelf, he followed her shadow as she tucked herself into bed.

Jack felt sure the other five members of the crew were asleep in their bunks. His father was sitting in a homemade wooden chair near the stove, keeping the fire stoked and watching the bread, should it become overdone and burn. Looking from his father to Molly's bunk, Jack saw that she had pulled back the screen to steal a glimpse of him.

He studied his father until he was sure he was solidly asleep in his chair. Relieved, he looked at Molly, who was also up on one elbow, mouthing something to him. In the dim light, he couldn't make out what she was saying. Jack checked on the old man again, and seeing he had gone off into a deep sleep with his head back on the chair, he motioned to Molly to come nearer, but with caution.

Molly poked her head out fully around the screen and also saw that the old skipper was asleep. She leaned a little farther toward Jack, reaching for him, and before she knew it he kissed her, the first time a man had ever kissed her! She put her hands around his face in the dim shade of the light and pulled him toward her, returning the kiss. They glanced at the skipper, and seeing him stir they quickly moved back into their own bunks and waited, smiling at each other.

Without warning, the old man jumped up and shook his head. The bread! He yanked open the hot oven door with his bare hands and peered at the pans of bread inside. "I must have dozed," he said, and looked toward the bunks. He sat back down and closed his eyes, mumbling, "Another few minutes."

Sleep was gone from the old man, and Jack knew it. Kissing Molly again was too big a risk, but he managed to reach out and squeeze her hand.

Jack grew up in the little town of Seldom-Come-By near Molly and her family and he had known her all his life. Her family thought the world of him, since he had always been a well-behaved youngster and become a man by taking his place in the fishing boat when he was fourteen years old. In the community he was a model teenager, even though he lived among some of the roughest and toughest men that ever went on the ocean. At eighteen, he still attended Sunday School when he was home, and so did Molly. But being a fisherman from the age of fourteen, away from the town every summer, Molly had seemed like a stranger to him when he returned in the fall, although he saw her almost every day when he returned.

Molly's parents had a large number of children, and living next door to Skipper Joe the two families spent a lot of time at each other's houses. It was because of this closeness that the crew picked Molly to be their cook for the summer down on the Labrador. She was the perfect girl. The skipper loved her almost as much as he loved any member of his own family, and Molly's family was confident he would guard her with his life.

The old skipper prayed in silence as he lay back in the homemade wooden chair. While he was wondering who would be holding the church services while he was away, he opened his eyes and caught a glimpse of something that didn't please him. In the shadows of the forecastle, there they were, Jack and Molly, holding hands! There could be no mistake. He snapped his eyes shut before they could see him looking. This behaviour could not continue, not on this schooner. It had to stop. With this thought, Skipper Joe Budden started coughing.

Startled by the old man's coughing fit, Jack and Molly quickly let go of each other's hands and rolled back in their bunks, thinking they had escaped detection. It was a close call.

I wonder what this voyage will bring forth, Skipper Joe thought as he waited for the batch of bread to bake.

TWO

The pier head at Yarmouth, England was busy as the little hospital boat *Albert* made ready to cross the broad Atlantic on June 15, 1892. She had undergone a refit, her sails had been changed, and she was all decked out with new canvas. The rudder was reinforced to withstand the strong winds and heavy currents she was certain to encounter while entering the mighty Arctic waters surrounding the great Canadian Shield. The captain was a Cornish man who ran his ships by a code of strict discipline on the high seas. He had taken his orders from the Honorary Agents of the Royal National Mission to Deep Sea Fishermen in London and would stray neither to the right nor the left until he delivered his ship and occupants to St. John's, Newfoundland. This captain's name was Joseph Trezise, and he was no stranger to the colony of Newfoundland and Labrador. He'd sailed their coasts on square-riggers and he knew the people well.

The *Albert* carried a crew of officers and crewmen, including a young man destined to become a giant among the medical pioneers of the world. For now he was the ship's physician. When he reached the New World, he would carry out the tasks assigned him by his superiors in London.

In December of 1886, an elderly Church of England clergyman in St. John's, Newfoundland by the name of Reverend Henry House had taken it upon himself to write the council of the National Mission to Deep Sea Fishermen in London, England. He had heard from many quarters of the callous behaviour of the fish merchants in Newfoundland and Labrador, and had experienced it first-hand. The fishermen and their families were suffering and dying at the hands of those who were unscrupulous. In his letter he asked that the Mission send medical personnel to work among the fishermen of Newfoundland, particularly those on the Grand Banks.

The Mission had met, and it was decided not to fulfill the request. Their organization was fully nondenominational, and therefore they would not become linked to any particular church or religion. However, concerned citizens and organizations in Newfoundland would not give up the cause, and many written entreaties were made for someone to come in the name of humanity. No one responded until 1891, when the council of the Mission to Deep Sea Fishermen sent Mr. Francis Hopwood, who was a member of the British Trades Council, on a working visit to Canada. While in Montreal, he decided he would visit the Newfoundland colony on his return to England.

When Hopwood arrived in St. John's, he was introduced to the great Newfoundland historian Dr. Moses Harvey, a prominent clergyman and a man who knew the ins and outs of every part of Newfoundland and Labrador and its people. He knew especially about the hardships continually being inflicted on the fishermen and their families by many of the fish merchants. Dr. Harvey introduced Mr. Hopwood to those people who could best describe to him the unbelievable hardships of the seasonal fishermen, particularly along the Great Northern Peninsula and the Labrador coast. There, families suffered untold personal poverty and disease, without hope, and were dying like sheep.

In the year 1891, the population of the colony of Newfoundland and Labrador was approximately 140,000 souls, with 3,400 of those living in Labrador. Mr. Hopwood learned that 30,000 fishermen, including women and children, left the island every spring to sail to the Labrador, where they prosecuted the fishery. The crowded conditions aboard the passenger vessels transporting fishing crews to the Labrador and the French Shore were nearly as brutal as the transatlantic slave trade.

Hopwood made careful notes during his briefings and observations and compiled them in a report. His report was submitted to the Mission, and its board reviewed his findings later that year.

This report was published in most major newspapers of the day in many countries, including Canada and the United States. It caused quite a sensation, prompting the Mission to Deep Sea Fishermen to respond to the Newfoundland outcry. Before the year ended, the governing body decided it would publish a request for a medical doctor to volunteer to go to Newfoundland and Labrador.

On the fifteenth day of June, 1892, a young applicant, Dr. Wilfred Thomason Grenfell, age twenty-seven, stepped on board the little sailing schooner *Albert*. He was full of vigour and possessed of boundless amounts of energy, eager to head out into the North Atlantic.

He held a master mariner's ticket, which was only to be used while sailing the yacht owned by a close friend of his, who was now an old man. Dr. Grenfell had gained some knowledge of the ocean and learned the meaning of "risk" after spending a couple of seasons in the North Sea, working with fishermen from Iceland to Norway. But his experience had been primarily with offshore fleets, and he knew things would be different in the New World.

The request said that medical assistance was needed along the shores of the Great Northern Peninsula and the Labrador coast. While the young doctor had some idea of what he would be doing, in his wildest dreams he could never imagine what he would experience in this part of God's creation.

And now on this day, standing on the deck of the *Albert* as it moved slowly out of the port of Yarmouth with the flags flying and the banners waving and the ship's horns screaming in his ears, young Dr. Grenfell headed out the harbour, bound for St. John's, Newfoundland.

There is nothing in the world as splendid as the sight of mighty icebergs, towering in a mirrorlike sea and lying in the shadows of walled cliffs made rugged by the pounding of the cruel North Atlantic. No other stretch of water is more cowardly and unforgiving than the Labrador Sea. Many lives has she swallowed up and destroyed, and with hurricanes and blizzards she has so gleefully accommodated, robbing men of their youth and shattering hopes and dreams of thousands of families. The deep, frigid water has bleached the bones of many who dared stand toe to toe with her and fight.

Skipper Joe Budden had high hopes as he came around Cape Bauld, which is situated on the northern end of Quirpon Island and off the tip of the Great Northern Peninsula. Far off to his right, looming in the midday sun, was an island called Belle Isle, with towering cliffs and fingers of snow reaching downward to the ocean, looking like the face of a half-starved vagabond after a hard winter.

Skipper Joe shaded his eyes and scanned the horizon. "Well, look at that."

"Look at what?" asked Fred.

The old man squinted in the sunlight. "I'd say there's a solid ice jam on the other side of the strait."

The other men followed the skipper's gaze.

"Something is looming up in the distance, sir," said Hap.

The skipper nodded. "Roy, go up in the rigging and have a look. You'll see better up there."

"Okay, Father," Roy said, moving to the other side of the schooner to climb the mast.

The sails flapped in the light wind, leaving one side of the schooner in shadows. Roy looked in all directions. "Yes, Father, it looks like there's a solid jam farther up ahead, and I don't see a hole of water anywhere."

Skipper Joe looked worried. He yelled up to Roy, "What's it like farther to the left and alongshore in the direction of L'Anse aux Meadows?"

"It looks like open water up along that way, but there are a lot of shoals there."

The skipper gave the wheel a spin and turned the schooner to the left as the crew tightened the yards. "We might go into Quirpon and see if anyone knows what the ice conditions are like in the strait. What do you think, men?"

The crewmen knew less about the area than the skipper so could offer no suggestions. They placed their trust in his judgment. Skipper Joe decided not to go into Quirpon and went on and trimmed the shoreline, taking care not to go aground on the many shoals. This was easy enough to do, and the old sea dog knew it, having passed along there many times before.

Going to the Labrador was sometimes, if not all the time, a very risky task. The only instrument used for navigation was the compass—no maps or charts had yet been made of that coast. Besides the compass, the captain needed several personal attributes: a natural instinct for direction and location; willpower; and steel nerves. Seafarers were at the mercy of the wind and tide, so added to these personal characteristics were two more: faith and skill. These would carry them safely to and from Labrador. The men who stood behind the wheels of those tiny homemade vessels were the best sailors in the world, self-made, hard-working, and daring. Many a man has stood on the deck in a raging storm and lived to sing the old standard, *Jack was every inch a sailor, five and twenty years a whaler, he was born upon the bright blue sea.*

Skipper Joe Budden, the captain of this small schooner, knew what hardship was all about. He knew well the risk and the perils of life, and as the light wind and strong tide pushed the schooner along with the keel just a few feet above the shoals, he conceded that they wouldn't get much farther. Finally, after coming too close to several shoals, he was forced to stop and drop anchors near L'Anse aux Meadows.

L'Anse aux Meadows is today a world-renowned national historic site. This is the place where a thousand years ago Leifr Eiriksson dropped anchor, but Skipper Joe Budden would never know that part of history. It wasn't until the early 1960s that Mr. George Decker, also a fisherman, led the great archaeologist Helge Ingstad to the Viking settlement there. In 1892, however, it had only a few dwellings and was a place where one could bide awhile, taking refuge from the grinding Arctic ice.

The skipper manoeuvred the little schooner through the loose ice pans, just a stone's throw away from the small houses sitting on the plateau by the sea. The tide was high, and he knew there was a chance that when it went out the vessel would lodge on the bottom. To make a run now for Quirpon wasn't possible, so the decision was made to stay where they were. The crew sounded the water until they found a deep hole safe enough to position the schooner. After putting out anchors and grapnels to prevent her from swinging with the tide, they retired for the night.

Around midnight the skipper roused the crew from their sleep. "I think we're aground, boys. It seems like she's listing to one side."

Each man was out of his bunk immediately and rushed to get dressed. As they came up on deck, they saw that the rear of the schooner was on the bottom. The tide was dead low, all the lines were tight, and there was no wind. They measured the depth of water, and, puzzled, found that there should be enough for the schooner to float in.

The skipper could sense everyone's concern. "There's not much we can do, only hope for the best. If we try and pull her off and there's a sharp rock touching her bottom, it could go right in through her."

The men agreed and moved quickly, putting the small rowboat overboard to permit Roy and Hap to inspect the bottom by torchlight.

"What does it look like?" asked the skipper.

"It seems like she's lodging on the rudder," Roy called, "but it's a job to see."

The men on deck lit another torch and handed it down, the flickering flame making the surface of the water loom up around the schooner.

Roy said, "The hull and keel aren't lodging on anything. It's just the rudder that's touching, and it's aground on a big round rock."

"That's not so good," said Skipper Joe. "With the weight of the schooner on it, the rudder shaft could push the casing up. If that happens, this thing will leak like a basket."

Bill, the skipper's oldest son, nodded in agreement. "The water should be dead low by now," he said.

The skipper looked at the salt-covered rocks that glistened in the moonlight on the shore. "There's not much we can do, only wait until the tide starts to rise and see what happens."

Molly came up on deck, and she looked a little frightened. "You can go back to bed," said Skipper Joe. "Don't worry. Everything will be all right."

"Okay, Skipper," she said.

He turned to the crew. "Jack, you and I'll take the first shift on deck—two hours. We'll keep watching in case she starts leaking or begins to swing around. After two hours, two more will come up and relieve us."

When the sun came up at five o'clock, everyone but Molly was on deck. No one had slept during the night.

Bill said, "The water is rising, Father, and in an hour or so she'll be afloat."

"Have you checked around the rudder case yet?" Skipper Joe asked.

"Yes, we have."

"And what did you find?"

"There's water running in."

"That's what I thought. How bad is it?"

"We don't know yet because she's still taking her weight," Bill said. "We'll know better when the tide gets higher and all the weight lifts off the rudder case."

Skipper Joe was worried they wouldn't be able to steer once the ship floated off the rock. "Do you think the rudder is broken?"

Bill shook his head. "No, the rudder looks okay to me."

"I think I know what happened," said the skipper. "When the weight came on the rudder, the pressure tore those two brass screws out of the counter knee. The rudder casing was pushed up, and that's where the water is coming in."

Bill nodded. "You're right. Remember what I told you when we installed it?"

The skipper remembered, all right. They had built this schooner from start to finish and had fastened her well, but there was one flaw in her that would not have been, had they listened to Bill.

"You're right, Bill. The next one we build, we'll change that."

Bill laughed. "It's too late now for this one. If that's what's wrong, you know what we have to do, don't you? We have to put her ashore and fix it."

Everyone listened quietly, knowing Bill was right.

Skipper Joe broke the silence. "We'll see how bad the leak is when she's floating, and that'll be very soon. Jack, you and Roy go down and cook some breakfast, but try not to wake Molly. She's been awake most of the night, so let her stay in the bunk until seven or eight."

"Okay," Roy and Jack said in unison, and descended into the forecastle.

The tide rose as usual, and the vessel floated off the rock. At 10:00 A.M., the schooner was moving across the Strait of Belle Isle in full canvas, ahead of a brisk southwest wind. She was leaking and had to be pumped every two hours, but this wouldn't stop Skipper Joe, because there was codfish in the traps at Cape Onion, a small settlement located on the headlands approximately six miles north of L'Anse aux Meadows. There were also reports of codfish in abundance along the Labrador coast. That was the only thing Skipper Joe Budden had on his mind as he skittered and wormed the little schooner through the rough ice—cod, the currency of Newfoundland.

After leaving Yarmouth, the *Albert* kept taking on water, so Captain Trezise took her to dock at Crookhaven, Ireland. No major problem was found, and the captain departed Ireland on July 4, back on course for St. John's, Newfoundland. In the early morning light of the eighteenth day out, the captain came on deck. Using his sextant, he got a fix on their latitude. He beckoned the mate, Joseph White, gave him the reading from the instrument, and White immediately went below to the chart room.

The captain looked over the railing at the vastness of the ocean, then up at the eastern sky, where the glow of the morning sun rested on the horizon. He judged that within an hour the small hospital ship would receive enough blessed warmth to free it from the previous night's chill.

White stepped up on deck again. "I have a fix on our position, Captain," he said.

"Yes, what is it?"

"We're dead on course. If all goes well, we should see land tomorrow afternoon."

"I guess this is the day we've been waiting for, and although we haven't broken any records, we've made pretty good time. What is the exact distance?"

White glanced at the piece of paper in his hand. "Right now we are one hundred and thirteen nautical miles from the harbour entrance of St. John's."

"Very good. Thank you, Joseph. It looks like we're going to have a great day."

"Yes, sir. We're having a perfect sunrise."

"Joseph," said Captain Trezise, "when the doctor gets up, please ask him to come to my room and have breakfast with me around eight o'clock."

"Yes, I certainly will, sir."

At the breakfast meeting, the young doctor, Wilfred Grenfell, talked about the Hopwood report and their plan of tackling such a problem.

"I guess there isn't much of a plan we can put in place, due to the fact that we have no facilities onshore," he said.

The captain said, "I think you're right, Wilfred. We'll have to play it by ear and hope for the best."

The young doctor said thoughtfully, "After we have a couple of days at St. John's and talk to some people, we might be able to get some direction."

"I was looking at one of the charts last night and noticed that there's a little settlement up there called Englee," said Trezise. "Maybe this is where we should make our first stop."

"That's a good idea," said Grenfell.

Breakfast was served and the two men talked as they ate. "We should see land sometime tomorrow, that is, if the wind doesn't pick up from the west. It does look like we'll have a westerly breeze, but I don't think it'll be too bad. But one thing's for sure, we won't be using any canvas, because we're going almost due west."

"Yes, you're right, Captain," said Grenfell. "The glass is in a perfect position. We should have a great day." With these words, Grenfell left, and Captain Trezise went for a mid-morning nap.

Around noon, the captain came on deck to relieve Robert Hewer at the wheel.

"How is everything, Robert?" he asked cheerfully.

"Not bad, but I think I've been on the sea too long," Hewer replied, grinning.

"Why do you say that?"

"Every once in awhile a strong scent drifts across my nose, like trees or firewood burning. Just now it was so strong I could have sworn that the front of the vessel was on fire. Maybe I'm dreaming, longing for landfall."

Captain Trezise laughed. "Well, Robert, I would say you're getting so close to land, as they say, that you can smell the blackberry bushes burning."

They both laughed, and as the captain took over the wheel, he said, "We're less than a hundred miles out now and on the home stretch."

A small gust of wind from the west made the canvas flutter as she pushed steadily on her course. Every man who came on deck remarked that he could smell something on the air. Grenfell came up on deck and made the same comment. He whistled and sang as the *Albert* slowly pushed its way through the clear waters. "Where are we now, Captain?" he asked.

"Half an hour ago I confirmed our position. We're going due west at five knots per hour, and we are approximately sixty-four miles east of St. John's harbour. By daylight tomorrow morning, if the weather stays like it is, we should be getting ready to enter the harbour of St. John's, Newfoundland."

The doctor laughed. "I guess, Captain, we will name it as John Cabot did, the 'New World.'"

"After being on a boat as long as this, any land is a new world," said Trezise.

They laughed.

As the sun sank in the glowing western sky, everyone on board had thoughts of tomorrow, the feeling of stepping onto the docks, and walking the streets of old St. John's. But quite a shock was awaiting the crew of the *Albert*, for as the small hospital schooner bobbed toward the harbour entrance, St. John's, North America's oldest European-settled city, was on fire and burning to the ground.

The *Albert* came through the narrows of St. John's on

the morning of July 23, 1892 and the city was still smouldering, the smoke and flying ash stinging the eyes of everyone on board. As the small hospital ship slowly approached the half-burned remains of a wharf, it became clear that its first job in the colony of Newfoundland would be to treat burn victims, in the worst conflagration ever to hit St. John's.

THREE

Skipper Joe Budden was a happy man when he dropped anchor at Battle Harbour, Labrador; it had been a rough trip across the Strait of Belle Isle. When the people of this little village found out where they had come from, they shook their heads and said that "only Skipper Joe could have done it," because the ice was so heavy. He was, they said, an extraordinary man.

The schooner was leaking badly. Skipper Joe talked to someone in Battle Harbour about putting her ashore at high tide to repair the rudder casing, but when he learned that there were lots of codfish around, he thought it best to chase them; the westerly wind was keeping the ice off, and as long as this was the case he would have to keep moving, even at night. The old-timers used to say that any captain who couldn't move around the Labrador coast at night had no business being there.

So the little schooner went on its way and edged along the coast, the light breeze just enough to make navigation easy. All eyes searched closely for any lurking hazard in front of them that could create a problem.

Molly lay on her bunk, fully clothed and ready to jump if need be. The forecastle was warm and dim with torchlight, and the kettle on the hot stove was singing in tune with the waves that rushed along the hull just inches from her face.

She was slowly but surely moving away from her home and family. Oh, how she missed her parents, especially her father. Molly knew he was thinking about her every minute. He had cried when he saw her walking down the narrow road from their house carrying the box in which she had stowed her belongings. Her father was a man who took his family to church every Sunday, and when Skipper Joe was away he would fill in for him and hold services, especially on Sundays, and she would assist him during those times.

However, Molly now had something else on her mind, and it was on her mind every moment. This something made her heart flutter. It was love, and the love that she felt wasn't the kind she had for her father and mother. It was for Jack, Skipper Joe's curly haired son.

"Yes," she whispered. "I'm in love with Jack."

She opened her eyes and looked for a moment at the flickering torchlight, reflecting on the wall as if it were someone dancing to a tune of joy. Jack's handsome face, the perfect daydream, smiled back at her. She had never felt like this before; it was the strangest feeling she'd ever had. She loved her parents because they were her providers and her protectors, but for Jack her love was different. Whenever she thought of him, her heart ached; if only she could be alone with him again. Maybe after they settled away on land she could steal away with him somewhere.

As Molly listened to the creaking sounds of wood, the splashing sound of the ocean, and the whistling of the steam from the kettle, her heart felt good. The motion of the boat gently rocked her to sleep and sent her to a dreamworld where Jack was her prince and she his princess.

In St. John's, Grenfell was thoroughly briefed by prominent and knowledgeable individuals such as historian Moses Harvey and Sir William Whiteway on Newfoundland and Labrador's social problems. He received a letter of support for his mission from Governor Terence O'Brien, and after days of giving medical attention to the victims of the fire in St. John's, Grenfell and the *Albert* left port. After several more days at sea, they encountered heavy ice. The vessel spent days stuck solid, unable to move, and when the ice slackened she could move only at a snail's pace. Finally, after weeks of battling the ice and strong currents, the *Albert* steamed into Englee, a small fishing settlement located at the mouth of Canada Bay, and founded by the French in the 1700s.

The vessel picked her way through rough ice and tied up to a wharf owned by a local fish merchant, Ralph Strong. By the time the lines were secured, the whole community had shown up to stare at the strangers. Dr. Grenfell's file describes the scene at the wharf in Englee.

> When we came to the wharf, there was no one to catch our lines. The crew secured the boat. We looked around for life, and finally we saw men coming our way. They were mere skeletons. In fact, some of them were staggering like drunken men, as if they were going to fall, and within ten minutes there was a whole lot of people on the wharf. I was surprised to find that they were all men.
>
> I went ashore and talked to them. I was told that people were beginning to starve, but I could see they had already been starving. It was a terrible sight. We got our stove out on the wharf and started cooking food. The men told us they were living on mussels they were getting along the shore until the herring came. There were no cod or even flatfish for them to catch, and there were cases of dysentery due to the contentious diet of herring.
>
> We distributed food around to them, as much as we could spare. The men of the town told us that they were oppressed by the fish merchants, that they would not supply the town for the winter with food because no fish had been caught the previous summer. They said there were no fish in the ocean.

Only God knows how many people died of starvation and were buried in unmarked graves. Hopwood's report rang true to the young physician. All that Sir Francis Hopwood had heard from Dr. Moses Harvey was true, and now Grenfell was beginning to see it for himself, right here on the Great Northern Peninsula.

What will it be like down on the Labrador? Grenfell wondered.

No one will ever know the real number of wrecks that litter the cold depths along the Labrador coast. Tales of bravery and sacrifice have been told and retold for generations, and many have faded from living memory. Skipper Joe Budden knew enough about the deadly shoals and ridges that lay as sleeping monsters underneath the surface of the briny ocean.

There was no sea heaving this night, due to the ice that lurked only a few feet away. His instructions to the crew were simple: "Keep her off a bit, boys," or "keep her in a ways."

The moon was rising and the wind was picking up. "'Tis going to be a great night for sailing," Skipper Joe said. "Conditions are just right. I had planned to go into Domino, but I don't think we will now. We'll go on outside, and if we can keep going all night we should be at Indian Tickle by tomorrow evening."

He looked at the tall spars towering above him and turned to check on the trap skiff in tow a hundred feet behind. Everything looked okay. "Roy, I want you, Hap and Gid to go below and get some sleep. Jack and I will take the first shift, along with Bill and Fred. Try not to wake Molly if you can do it. Unless there's trouble, I won't wake you 'til our three hours are up."

Everyone acknowledged the orders, and the three men went below.

"Jack," said the skipper, "I want you to give the schooner a good pumping and make sure all the water is out of her. When that's done you can turn in 'til five o'clock. When Molly gets up you can help her get breakfast."

"Okay, Father," Jack said. "Are you sure you don't need me?"

"We'll be fine here. Just make sure all the water is out first."

"All right," said Jack, and he went directly to the pump. The other two men stood on watch with the skipper. Their voices carried back and forth to one another on the wind, and the only other sounds were the running water along the sides, the soft, light breeze in the rigging, and the occasional squeak of the pump.

"She's dry," Jack said finally.

"Thanks," said Skipper Joe. "You can go below and get some rest. It's been a long day."

"Thanks, Father." Jack knew it would be no use for him to offer to stay up so his father could take a rest; only Roy or his father would be on deck in charge at night. He turned and disappeared down the companionway toward the fore-castle.

The *Albert* twisted and heaved as it shouldered its way through the rough ice. The hull stood solid against the pressure as the boat rose partway out of the water and ground its way through the ice pans. The vessel had been battering heavy ice for four days and nights, and finally she was nearing open water close to land.

Captain Trezise knew at once where he was; he had been here before. They were close to Battle Harbour, Labrador, a place where fish merchants made their Labrador headquarters during the summer season before shutting everything down in the fall and moving to St. John's for the winter. They would live in luxury in the city while the local residents who made them rich were forced to live off the land and exist on the meagre foodstuffs sent their way. Those residents lived like dogs, feeding from the bones that were thrown to them.

Dr. Grenfell came on deck. Looking at the land in the distance, he could see snow high on the hills. "Where are we now, Captain?" he asked, knowing they were somewhere near Labrador.

"See that group of islands? Well, in among them is our destination, Battle Harbour."

"Will we be there tonight?"

Captain Trezise squinted in the midday sun as he looked past the Battle Harbour islands. "I don't know. It looks to me like there's a solid ice jam on the inside of those islands, so we'll try and get some information when we get into the harbour. We'll try and take on some fresh water if the source is fairly close, since we have only a tierce and a half left. It could take a nice bit of time to get the water on board, so I daresay we'll stay there overnight."

"Why, that's good, Captain, thank you. I'll hold a clinic as soon as we get there."

"I guess that's what you came here for, Doc," Trezise said with a smile.

"That's right," said Grenfell, any nervousness he'd once felt now overpowered by an eagerness to get the job done.

From overhead, the man in the rigging called down to the deck. "Captain! Hello, Captain!"

"Tell him that I can hear him," Trezise said to one of the sailors standing next to him.

The sailor cupped his mouth with his hands and yelled back. "What is your message for the captain?"

The lookout called, "There's a large pan of ice across the channel. It looks impossible for us to get into the harbour, but it appears we can go on outside."

"It must be a flat pan," the captain muttered. "Tell the mate to keep her off," he said to the man beside him.

The crewman followed his orders, and Captain Trezise watched as the *Albert* took a slow turn outward.

"I wonder if we can get in through the outside tickle," he said to the messenger, but before he could respond, the man in the rigging called down again. "Tell the captain that I see a small fishing boat near the shore on the port side."

Everyone looked to the left.

"There it is, over there," a deckhand said as he pointed.

Sure enough, there it was, a small boat.

Captain Trezise stared out the port side. "Tell the mate to turn the vessel over toward the fishing boat. We may get information about the ice conditions from them."

"Aye, sir."

The captain told his crew to begin signalling to the men in the boat. After a few minutes, the strangers saw the signal and started waving back; they let their net go and began rowing toward the vessel. As they approached, it became obvious that these locals were fishermen.

"Hello," they called.

The crew of the *Albert* greeted the strangers as they brought the small boat to a stop alongside. "Are you men from Battle Harbour?" a crewman asked.

"Yes, we are," one of the fishermen replied.

Captain Trezise moved over to the rail and looked down. At first glance he knew what they were doing: hauling their salmon nets. "Are you men familiar with the ice conditions farther north along the coast?"

"No," they replied. "Only around here."

"I see," said the captain. "We're going farther north if the ice permits us—we are a hospital ship."

The three fishermen looked at the captain, then at the *Albert* itself. One of them said, "I told the boys that your ship looked unusual for one of those fish merchants. Looks like I was right."

"What's it like getting into the harbour?"

"You won't get in there now."

"Well, we want to go into Battle Harbour, because the doctor here would like to hold a medical clinic. We'd planned to take on some fresh water, too."

The three fishermen looked at the crew with great interest, and one finally spoke. "The ice was gone for awhile. We trapped a lot of fish but had to take our gear out of the water because it returned, and we decided to go salmon-catching instead. Would you like to have some, sir?"

Trezise's mouth watered when he looked at the large salmon in the boat. He couldn't turn down such a delicacy. "Yes, we certainly would."

"How many?"

"We could use a couple."

A man in the boat threw his painter to one of the sailors aboard the *Albert*, and the crewman immediately pulled it closer.

"Lower down your tub."

A tub was lowered, and one man held it while the others put in a dozen of their largest salmon.

"Hoist her away," the fishermen said.

The captain insisted he didn't want to take that many salmon from them, but his protest was to no avail.

"How much do we owe you?" Captain Trezise asked.

"Don't mention it. We've never charged anyone yet, especially for a salmon."

"Just a minute." He turned around and spoke to Grenfell briefly, and the doctor sent two sailors below to fetch something. When they came back up they were carrying two boxes, and they passed them down to the fishermen.

"Any of you smoke?" asked the captain.

"Yes!" was the unanimous cry.

"Well, here." He threw down a tin of loose tobacco and two sticks of Black Beaver chewing tobacco.

The three fishermen were delighted to receive such a treat. After they thanked Captain Trezise for his generosity, the *Albert* spread her sails and left the three men with their fortune.

Dr. Grenfell watched as the fishermen rowed toward shore. "You know, Captain, this was our first encounter with people on this shore, and it proves what Dr. Moses Harvey said. 'You will find the Labrador people to be the best people in the world.'"

Captain Trezise nodded. "That's what he said. And he's right."

It was June 10, 1892 when Skipper Joe Budden dropped anchor among the small islands of Indian Tickle, Labrador. He had been out thirteen days from Seldom-Come-By, Notre Dame Bay, and finally arrived at the place where he would spend the summer with his crew, fishing for cod. Here the ice had moved off, there was a good swell on the water, and the weather was muggy.

The skipper had no established premises on the Labrador; he went wherever there were reports of fish, preferably away from the populated areas, and there he would erect a simple tarpaper shack and a small stage and stagehead. Skipper Joe salted his fish on board the schooner and dried it on land before shipping it home to Newfoundland for market. Most years he made two trips.

In Indian Tickle there were hundreds of gulls flying close to the water. As Skipper Joe looked out over the ocean, he mused, "She sure looks fishy-looking. I wonder if there's anything worth jigging?"

He called to Roy. "Let's a couple of us row out to the trap berth and see if there's any fish. We may get a couple to make a feed of fish and brewis."

"A good idea, Father. The signs are good."

"You never know. We arrived here earlier than this once and caught fish, so I think it's worth a try."

Roy thought so too. "There's nothing wrong with trying."

The skipper turned to Jack. "We're going outside to have a try for a fish, so I want you to stay here with Gid and pump out the bilge water every two hours. Start getting our supplies ashore, too. We shouldn't be gone long."

"Okay, Father. Don't worry about a thing."

Jack and Gid loaded the cod jiggers aboard and launched the trap punt as the skipper and the others pushed off to investigate the grounds for a suitable trap berth. Two sets of oars made the skiff move with the grace of a swan, and Skipper Joe and the others were soon out the harbour and out of sight.

"Gid," said Jack, "what does Father plan to do, I wonder? Does he intend to put the schooner ashore first and fix the leak?"

"Jack, my son, listen," Gid said. "Don't you know what will happen if you put this schooner ashore with all the weight aboard? When the water falls, she could tip bottom-up and punch a hole in her and break off the planks."

"You're right, Gid. I never thought of that."

Gid shrugged. "I'm going ashore to take a look and see if there's a deep enough space to land our gear, so you can stay aboard with Molly."

He grinned, and before Jack could answer, Gid added, "No hanky-panky, my son."

He laughed as Jack started to blush.

Gid jumped down into the punt while Jack walked over to the deck pumps and started working the handle. Molly came up on deck from the forecastle, emerging in a long, light green dress and white homemade apron. In her arms was a bucket half-filled with dishwater. She walked over to the bulwarks and dumped the contents overboard. Jack watched her as he worked the pumps, and she could feel his eyes on her as she put the bucket down.

Molly lifted her dress to her knee and brushed her leg as if there had been something splashed on it. Jack lost a few strokes of the pump but continued at a slower pace. Molly laughed and walked toward him.

"Jack," she said in a soft, pleasant voice, "don't you love it here on the Labrador? I mean, look at the hills with the streaks of snow, and the deep blue of the sky. The air smells so fresh."

Jack looked admiringly at Molly as she edged closer to him. He saw the gleam in her eye, and his heart started pounding as he pumped the water from the boat. He wasn't interested in the blue of the sky or the streaks of snow on the hills. His only interest was Molly.

"Jack, all the water is out of the schooner, I think," she giggled.

Jack looked from Molly to the pump handle and let it go, wincing self-consciously when it hit the deck. Clearing his throat, he said, "Well, well, Molly, you're looking as if you just stepped out of your mother's kitchen. I guess the trip from home to the Labrador has had no effect on you; it's only made you look more beautiful."

Molly took another step toward him, and Jack gave a nervous glance toward the shore in Gid's direction. He couldn't see him, but Jack knew he was in the immediate area. All of a sudden, he reached out for Molly and pulled her close for a kiss.

"I love you," Molly said.

Jack was shaken. He didn't want Gid to see them alone, and he was afraid his father would find out. "You'd better go on down into the forecastle, Molly. I don't want Gid to see us alone, especially kissing." His voice cracked at the last word.

"Jack, before I go, tell me what 'hanky-panky' means." She grinned.

"I suppose it means you and me drinking tea down in the forecastle together."

"Are you hungry, Jack? Do you want a lunch?" she teased.

"Not yet. Gid needs me ashore." Jack wanted to follow her down into the galley, but he had just caught sight of his partner on the shoreline.

Molly also spotted Gid. She disentangled herself from Jack's arms and went below alone.

Skipper Joe and his crew rowed for half an hour to the trap berth. It had been ten years since they'd been at this particular spot, but the skipper knew the marks.

"We hauled the fish up here one time, boys. For three weeks it was load and go, and this looks like the same kind of year."

"I hope you're right," said Roy. "We'll be needing it."

The skipper let his jigger sink to the bottom. "You know something, boys? I think I struck a fish on the way down."

Everyone watched him as he made one jig. "Yes, I struck one, or I struck something." He was excited. "Yes, I got something on. It's a codfish—I can tell by the feel of it."

"Father," said Bill, chuckling, "you'd better be careful. You're a Christian man, you know. You better not be telling lies, now. That could be a johnny sculpin." A johnny sculpin is a small fish that lives near the shoreline and is considered the king of scavengers.

"Johnny sculpin my eye! Look, just look at that coming up." The five men laughed as Skipper Joe lifted a twenty-pound codfish in over the boat.

"I could kiss you this morning," he said as the fish twisted on the hook, its mouth gaping wide as if gulping for air.

The skipper was bubbling with excitement. He said, "We have to give God thanks for this, you know."

"Not 'til I get one first," Roy laughed.

"Be careful, Roy, my son. The Man above controls all this, you know." His statement fell on deaf ears, because each man was now concentrating on hauling in codfish.

After a few minutes, Roy looked around. "Don't jig any more, boys," he said. "We have enough for supper, so let's head back for the cod trap. If we get the trap and moorings out it'll also lighten the schooner, and this evening we'll be able to put her ashore."

Skipper Joe nodded in agreement, and they headed back to No Man's Cove to begin their work for the summer.

Jack and Gid were landing lumber at the spot onshore where they would build their summer fishing shack. They had been working for two hours since the skipper's departure, and they were sweating from their exertions. Gid was only twenty years old, but he had proven himself by taking on responsibility for almost any job, so he had been chosen to decide where and how to construct their fishing stage and temporary cabin on land. He had done this for several years, although he was young and only in his seventh year on the Labrador. He was a powerful young man, hard-working, and had never been in any trouble in his life.

He came from a good family of noble fishermen. When Gid was fifteen years old, his father had been killed on a return trip from the Labrador when they got caught in a September gale. They were close to Belle Isle when they decided to take in some of the canvas, and in doing so Gid's father was struck in the head with the mainboom. It had come loose when a block broke, and suddenly swung across the schooner, killing the man instantly. Shortly after that, Gid hooked a job with Skipper Joe Budden and stayed with him ever since.

This trip, however, was different than all the others. There was a problem. A young woman was aboard, and both Gid and Jack were in love with her. Jack was eighteen, two years younger than Gid, and they were the best of friends, working and eating together and sharing a bunk in cramped quarters. Both had their eyes on Molly and were waiting for the chance to sneak down into the forecastle with her.

Jack was unaware that Gid had his eye on Molly, and he also didn't realize that Gid saw everything that passed between the two lovebirds. They flirted and held hands, stole kisses in the darkened shadows of the forecastle, and Jack thought the only person he had to look out for was his father.

As the two young men worked at the lumber, Jack looked up. "Listen. I can hear the old man singing."

Gid stopped working and turned his ear to the sound. He nodded. Sure enough, the others were on their way back into the harbour.

"Listen, Gid, 'tis the old man, all right. One of two things has happened. He either just came out of a church service or he struck fish."

"I doubt it very much that with Roy aboard they went to a church service out there today," Gid said, laughing.

Jack grinned. "Then they must have struck the fish."

The two young men pushed their small boat away from the beach and rowed off toward the schooner to meet the others.

FOUR

The crew were excited as they cleaned the fish. "'Tis thousands," said Hap. "You can't get the jigger to the bottom." "And the biggest kind," said Roy.

Listening to the men, Molly felt excited at being a part of the whole operation. This also meant she was going to get paid. She stood near Jack, who was asking his father questions about the fish and the depth of the water.

"Skipper," she said, "I have dinner all ready—stewed beans—so you can come and have it now. You must be hungry."

"You're a good girl, Molly," Skipper Joe said, and he was pleased to see this beautiful girl standing near his son. Since they left home, he hadn't found one fault in her. She was up early in the mornings, baked excellent bread, and kept the place spotlessly clean. Molly laughed and sang, morning and night, and she didn't get seasick.

"Boys," the skipper said, "let's go and have dinner."

The crewmen voiced their agreement and went below, but Jack didn't join them right away. He went directly to the pump. It had been two hours since he last pumped.

"I'm glad you thought about that," said his father. He came over and pounded Jack's shoulder with affection.

"I won't be long," said Jack. "Don't eat all the beans."

"You'll get your share," his father said, laughing as he followed the hungry crew into the forecastle.

Skipper Joe and the crew ate their stewed beans in a hurry, and he spoke as they sat around the table. "Men," he said, "we're going to put the cod trap out this afternoon. I know there's a lot of ice around, but there's a lot of fish, too."

Roy swallowed a mouthful of beans. "You're right about the ice and the fish, Father, but don't you think we should wait a couple of days to see what the ice might do?"

"I don't know, but one thing's for sure. There's lots of fish, and that's what we're here for. I've never seen anything caught yet without taking a risk for it."

Roy looked concerned. "But is it worth it, Father? I mean, is it worth losing a cod trap for a couple of loads of fish?"

The skipper reconsidered. "Maybe we'll put it out in the mornings and take it up again in the evenings."

"Well, I suppose we could do that, although it'll be a lot of hard work. The work part we don't mind, if we can get a load of fish a day."

"That would be perfect," the skipper said between bites.

"What about this leaky basket we're in?" Hap asked. "This thing has to be pumped every two hours, you know."

Skipper Joe agreed. "We'll have to leave Jack on board to pump her, and the first chance we get we'll put her ashore."

They had almost finished eating when Jack came down and sat at the table. "What's the word, Father?" he said as he tackled a plateful of Molly's beans.

"We're going to put the trap out."

"When?"

"This afternoon," Roy interrupted, "but you're going to stay here and keep this basket afloat."

Jack nodded. It made sense to leave him aboard. Someone had to do it, after all.

"Between the pumping, I want you to get as much of the remaining gear ashore as possible," said Skipper Joe.

Gid spoke up. "We have the floor of the cabin down, Skipper."

"Good work."

"It won't take us long to stick up the walls and put the roof on when we get onshore," Gid continued.

"I'll help Jack," Molly offered.

"Yes, it might be all right for you to get ashore for awhile," said the skipper. "But be careful. The rocks along the beach are slippery, and you might slip and hurt yourself."

"I'll watch out," she said.

Skipper Joe dropped his fork and stood up. "Okay, boys," he said, "let's start hauling the trap into the boat. The moorings have to go on top. It's the first thing that has to go out."

Roy looked at his father. "I guess we'll have to take the twelve-fathom trap. It looks like we'll need the thirty-five-fathom leader, too, according to the water and the distance from shore."

In a very short time, the skipper and crew rowed the twenty-eight-foot trap skiff out the harbour, leaving Jack and Molly alone for the first time.

The *Albert* wasn't as lucky in escaping the ice as Skipper Joe Budden and his little schooner had been.

"It's a late year," said Captain Trezise, meaning the ice was late in clearing away from the fishing grounds.

From his perch attached to the mast, the barrelman shouted down to the skipper, "The ice is as far as the eye can see."

The captain ordered the vessel to stop.

The mate said, "The tide appears to be keeping the ice pinned against the land in this area, and it looks like we're in for a southeaster, according to the glass."

"Lewis's Bay is full of ice," Captain Trezise said. "That's why we couldn't get into Battle Harbour."

He knew that bad weather was on the way, and between the land and a field of ice was no place to be caught. He had to make a decision. "Set a course to the southwest and put all the canvas on her. We'll run for five hours; this should take us well across the strait and close to Brandy Harbour, depending on the ice, of course."

"Okay," said the mate, and proceeded to get the *Albert* out of the ice and under full sail. The wind from the southeast was picking up already.

Dr. Grenfell came on deck and the captain informed him of what was happening. Although he was disappointed, Grenfell was certain the captain knew what he was doing. Trezise was a cautious old sea dog and had every right to make the sailing decisions on the *Albert*.

Maybe I'll get ashore at Brandy Harbour and hold medical clinics there, Grenfell thought.

It was unfortunate that they wouldn't get into Battle Harbour this time around, but in a few days they would move on farther north again and visit then.

The sun tried to break through the clouds as Jack put the handle into the shank end of the pump and worked it up and down with a smooth motion. He was a strong young man, and his blazing red hair swayed with the rhythm of his pumping, up and down. Molly had come up out of the forecastle and watched the trap skiff disappear around the point.

"Let me help you, Jack," she said as she reached for the handle. Jack slowed down enough for her to get into the motion of the pumping. "Here we go," she said. "I like this."

They pumped for ten minutes, until a sucking sound indicated that the water was out.

"It's all out, Jack," said Molly playfully, flirting with him as they pumped. "Let's go ashore on this great Labrador."

"Hey," Jack said, "that rhymes. We'll go ashore on Labrador." They giggled. It was a wonderful moment for them both. Jack put his arms around her, and they kissed.

39

"You'd better clean up the dishes down below, Molly."

"All right, Jack. While you get the boat ready and the stuff on board, I'll do my work in the galley."

"Better still, Molly, I'll help you with your work first, and after that you can help me do mine."

"Okay," she said, and as she turned to go down below, she added, "What about your father's orders, Jack?"

Jack pretended not to hear as he walked past her and disappeared down below into the galley.

Molly didn't like to disobey orders, and Jack was Skipper Joe's son. Looking around at the schooner and at the rocky hills beyond, she felt as if there were eyes watching her. She looked at her hands. They were sweating.

Jack called to her from below. "Hey, Molly, come on down."

She rubbed her sweaty palms in her apron and thought about what the skipper had told her. *When I'm not around, don't allow anyone into the galley, especially when you're alone.*

Jack called again. "Hey, Molly! Come on down and let's get this mess cleaned up."

Molly glanced around at the shore and the hills beyond. "Oh, yes, the mess," she murmured, as if waking from a deep sleep.

"I'm coming, Jack," she called, and she darted into the companionway.

The voice followed her as she turned around and climbed down the ladder, feeling Jack's hands guiding her down into the galley.

You'll be sorry, Molly, Skipper Joe's voice echoed in her mind.

FIVE

The *Albert* spent four days at Quirpon Island. She had been unable to get into the Cooks Harbour area and instead had gone to the little settlement of L'Anse au Pigeon, near Cape Bauld. Historians say that at one time Quirpon Island was the Eskimo (Inuit) capital of the eastern seaboard, and according to the writings of Sir Joseph Banks, Quirpon was the most active area in the north. Legend has it that this island is also the place where the Sieur de Roberval put his niece ashore for having an affair with a French cavalier.

Most of the pack ice had moved farther off, yet numerous icebergs still littered the sea, even now in August. When the storm cleared and the ice let the *Albert* out, she set sail for Battle Harbour again. However, Captain Trezise was determined to take it farther north. "We've had a late year, Doctor," he said.

"We certainly have," Grenfell said, pointing to a spot on the map. "Let's head for here, Captain."

"I thought you said you wanted to head straight for Domino Run."

"Yes, but maybe we should touch into this little town, Snug Harbour, and have a look at the people. I have a feeling they need us."

41

"We'll see."

"Good," said the young doctor.

In less than five hours, they neared the entrance to Snug Harbour. A huge iceberg towered in the gleaming sunlight at the mouth of the little harbour, and as the lazy sea licked at its sides, it gave off a crackling sound, like breaking glass. The little hospital ship squeezed by the iceberg and entered the harbour. The anchor was dropped, making a loud chinking noise as the chain ran out through the hawse pipe, and the canvas flapped in the light westerly wind as the crew prepared to take it in.

When the schooner was secured, the captain and his crew stood at the railing, surveying the small houses and huts onshore. Women and children stood outside their doorways, staring at the schooner in the harbour. Small stages perched on stilts along the rocky shoreline, the boats tied to the stagehead were laden with codfish, and men were busying themselves with splitting and salting their catch.

As the crew of the *Albert* watched this picturesque scene, they heard a woman's voice calling from inside one of the small houses.

"Silas! Hey, Silas!" the woman called.

Following a lengthy pause, a man onshore said, "Peter, see what your mother wants."

Peter called out to the woman. "Yes, Mother, what do you want Father for?"

"Do you see that schooner there in the harbour?" the young man's mother asked.

Peter and the others stared at the strange schooner moored in the harbour, a hundred feet from the stagehead. He looked at the men around him. "The old woman must think we're all gone to sleep down here." He raised his voice and said, "No, Mother. What schooner are you talking about?"

The men laughed at the little joke as Silas came out of the stage and into the bright sunlight. He shaded his eyes with his hand, and for the first time he saw the *Albert*.

"Yes, my dear," he called to his wife, "we see it. And a strange one it is."

"I wonder where it came from?" said the woman.

The men onshore walked to the front of the wharf to get a closer look, arguing with each other and debating whether the strange ship was a banker or a floating merchant. The crew of the *Albert* looked closely at the faces of the men onshore. Most of them were thin, dirty boys.

"These people don't seem to have much weight on them, Doctor," Captain Trezise said. "I bet you could do a lot of business here."

"It looks that way," Grenfell replied without taking his eyes off of the men on the beach.

"Are you ready to go ashore and start your clinic?"

"Yes, and I'd like one of your first aid men to accompany me, if you please."

"Yes, indeed." The captain turned to his crew. "Let down the boat, men."

In a few minutes, two oarsmen, the young doctor, and his assistant were rowing toward the nearest wharf.

"Harry," said Grenfell, "I hope that within the next few minutes we'll be making history."

The doctor's assistant, Harry Taylor, looked at him. "What do you mean?"

"As far as I know, this is the first time an English doctor has ever set foot on the Labrador. What do you think?"

"Maybe you're right."

The boat came to the makeshift wharf, which was constructed of poles and slabs of wood fastened by nails and looked as if it would collapse at any moment. The fishermen stood by to help the men up, and they were greeted by Silas, the shore skipper, a man who appeared to be well over sixty years of age, with his long, bony face and dark complexion. His huge hands were covered in coarse salt, the scars of hard toil showing through, but the man's deep blue eyes appeared soft and gentle.

"Hello, sir," Silas said to the doctor in a thick Labrador accent. The young doctor surmised that this man was a permanent livyer of Labrador.

"Hello," Grenfell echoed.

"You appear to be strangers to Labrador, sir."

"Yes, we are. In fact, this is our first time ever setting foot on Labrador soil."

Silas wiped the salt from his right hand and held it out. "Welcome to Labrador. I'm Silas." The man's leathery face cracked into a smile as the young doctor caught his hand.

"How are you, Silas? I'm Dr. Wilfred Grenfell, and this is my assistant, Harry Taylor. I've come to spend the summer on the Labrador coast, working around fisherfolk. I represent the Mission to Deep Sea Fishermen, out of England."

Silas stood as if frozen, not speaking, then he turned away. Grenfell and Taylor looked at each other. Silas turned back to them, and the young doctor was surprised to see tears running down his face, clear like rainwater. It seemed they had touched the very heart of this man.

The men and boys from the other stages crowded around them, and Silas spoke with some difficulty, choking on his words. "You were sent here by God, Doctor."

As Silas's tears of joy fell in the afternoon sun, Grenfell's soul was watered and fed, because this man believed he could make a difference. The young doctor felt tears of his own come to his eyes, tears of empathy and great love.

Silas shook his head. "Doctor," he stammered, "I have a little girl dying at my house. I'm a Christian and I prayed that the Lord would send us a miracle. Can you come and see my little girl?"

"Yes, I certainly can."

Silas removed his homemade work apron. He washed his hands in a bucket of salt water nearby and said to the men around him, "Okay, boys, you know what to do. I'll be back as soon as I can." With these words, he led the doctor and his assistant to his house.

A boardwalk led to the small bungalow. The building was made to endure the cold weather. It was constructed with a low ceiling, six and a half feet high, and had small, double windows and a heavy door to protect the people inside from the elements. Silas's wife was outside near the door, using her hand to shade her eyes from the glare of the hot sun. Her dark clothes were neat and clean and protected by a long, white apron.

Silas looked at his wife, who appearead as surprised as he was. "Mag, I have the answer to our prayers here with me."

The woman who had been calling to Peter onshore held out her hands and smiled. "Who is it, Silas?"

"This is a doctor. He was on that schooner out there."

"Oh, my," she gasped.

"I'm Dr. Grenfell, and this is my assistant. I understand you have a sick child."

"Yes, we do," Mag blurted. "Please come in."

The smell of baking bread greeted them as they bent their heads to get through the door of the modest but clean hut. The furniture was homemade, and the walls, ceiling and floor were just bare boards that had been scrubbed white.

"Our little girl is nine years old, Doctor," said Mag.

"How long has she been sick?" Grenfell asked, removing his jacket and placing his medical bag on the table.

"She has been sick now for two weeks," Silas answered.

"Has she eaten anything in that time?"

"Not very much. Only a little broth, which she threw up."

Grenfell looked around. "Where is the child?"

Mag stepped into an adjoining room and the young doctor followed her, leaving Silas and Harry in the kitchen.

The room was as hot as an oven. Grenfell strode over to the bed in a businesslike manner. He found that the little child had a high fever and was semi-conscious. He took her temperature, and after a more thorough examination he gave a diagnosis.

"This child has appendicitis," he said to the mother.

The heat in the cramped room was stifling. Grenfell came out to where Silas was sitting. "My dear man, you are killing your child and you don't even know it! You have to get that window open in the bedroom."

Silas turned white with shock. Never in his life had he dreamt of doing anything to hurt his child.

"The child has such a high temperature that her fever and the heat in the room could result in brain damage. Get that window open immediately!"

"I certainly will, Doctor." Silas stood, knocking his chair back as he did so. He darted through the doorway.

Grenfell went back into the room again to reassess the child's condition, this time with Taylor at his side. The doctor gestured to him, and they both went back out to the kitchen.

"She has a bad case of appendicitis, Harry. I'm not sure how far the poison has gone."

Taylor shook his head. "It's hard to tell, but she doesn't look like a hopeless case. I'd say there's only one remedy."

"Maybe you're right," Grenfell said.

"Her blood pressure appears to be very low. Do you think we could get her aboard the boat?"

"I don't think so. We could do a lot of damage by moving her. What is to be done has to be done here."

"Okay, you can do it."

"I like your confidence," Grenfell said.

"We don't have any other choice, do we, Doctor?"

"Would you call the mother out, please? I'll have a talk with her and tell her that we have to operate. We'll see if she agrees."

"Okay," said Taylor, and he went into the bedroom.

Silas came back in the kitchen. He had taken the storm window out of the tiny bedroom.

"Now, open the outer window, please," Grenfell said.

"Yes, sir, but I'll have to take the glass out."

Grenfell was firm. "That room must be ventilated."

Silas immediately set about removing the glass.

Mag stepped into the kitchen. Dr. Grenfell informed her that the child had appendicitis and would have to be operated on immediately. She was frightened, of course, and when Silas stepped back inside, the doctor outlined the procedure to both of them.

"Do you want some time to talk it over in private?"

Mag and Silas looked at each other. Silas cleared his throat and said, "No, Doctor. We give our consent."

"You made the right decision," said Grenfell. "First, let me say that I don't want anyone in the house for twenty-four hours, except for the four of us. You'd better tell the rest of the family. We will need lots of hot water."

He turned to Taylor and said, "You'll have to stay here while I go to the schooner and get my surgical kit."

The young doctor then drew a diagram and explained to Mag and Silas the procedure he was about to perform.

Dr. Grenfell worked as quickly as possible to remove the inflamed appendix from the girl. In short order, he removed the infected tissue and stitched the girl back up. When he put the child back into bed, he thanked his assistant and sat down at the table while Taylor headed back to the *Albert*.

Silas brought a steaming cup of tea to the doctor and sat across from him. Grenfell thanked him and sipped the beverage. "What's it like here in the winter, Silas?" he asked.

"It's not very good," Silas said, "especially last winter." He stared at his calloused hands. "Last summer the ice didn't leave the coast until the end of July, and by that time the fish had been here and gone. We couldn't get our fishing gear in the water. When the merchants came in September, there was next to no fish for them, so they left quicker than they came, leaving this place with twelve families and not one of them with enough food for the winter. Some didn't have any. The fish merchants wouldn't part with any of the goods unless we had fish to put in their hands, and we just didn't have it."

Dr. Grenfell looked at him with curiosity. "What did the people do? How did they survive?"

Silas gripped the edge of the table and looked down at the floor. "Doctor," he mumbled, "there's a story that I have to tell you, and the reason I'm telling you is maybe you could tell it to someone else, perhaps even to the governor."

Dr. Grenfell held up a finger, motioning for Silas to hold his thoughts. He went in and checked on the child, then came back and sat down, requesting that Silas continue. Unable to contain his emotions as he thought about the events he had witnessed, Silas laid his head on his arm and sobbed uncontrollably. Ashamed, he took a handkerchief from his overalls pocket and covered his face.

Grenfell reached over and laid a hand on the man's shoulders. "My dear man," he whispered, "your little girl will be all right in a couple of days, so you can stop crying."

"Doctor, I'm not crying over my little girl; I know now that she'll be all right. You're the answer to our prayers. I'm thinking about what happened last winter. We're still broken-hearted, and I guess we'll never get over it."

Dr. Grenfell looked at Silas in puzzlement. He could see pain in the skipper's eyes, pain such as he'd never seen before. "Go on, Silas," he said. "Tell me what happened."

Silas began. "My brother's name was Nicholas and his wife's name was Annie. He and two other families lived just up from here, about a mile away. Silas and Annie had four children, a son, John, who was the oldest—he was fourteen—and three little girls, the youngest four years old. Now, Nicky was a hard worker. He was the first man up in the morning and the last to bed in the night. But he was cursed like us all, Doctor.

"We're all cursed because we're slaves to the fish merchants, under their control and at their mercy, or at least that's how it seems. If they don't like us they can get rid of us by starving us, and we don't have anyone to turn to. The government doesn't care—they *are* the government."

Silas wiped his wrinkled face. "As I told you, last summer the fishery was a total failure. When the floating merchants came in here and we had no fish to give them, they just up and left without advancing an ounce of food. They told us that if they gave us the food they wouldn't have anything left to bargain with anyone else on the coast and would have to go back to St. John's empty-handed. We begged them, but they just cast off their lines and left hungry children standing on the wharf. And Doctor, I tell you, to see that boat leave here with lots of food on board, and to see hungry people standing on the wharf, that was a sad thing.

"Well, after it left, we all met—the men, that is—and tried to figure out what we should do. We knew that the only thing we could do was live off the land, but this wasn't likely because we're not trappers or hunters. Nicky was the most worried person of all the crowd, because he had the least in his pantry and cellar. We figured we'd get some fish in the fall, but the blowy weather came on early and we couldn't get out in the boat, not even to shoot birds. To cap it all, in November we had a terrible storm that swept the Labrador coast, and all our wharves and stages were swept away. By Christmas, every sheep and goat in the place was killed and eaten and our dogs all starved.

"New Year's Eve, Nicky came here and told us that he was hungry. He never had a bit of food to give his family, so we gave him five pounds of flour and a couple of pounds of rolled oats, and we told him that it was half of what we had. 'Well, Silas,' he said to me, 'I'm not going to wait and watch my wife and children starve. I just haven't got the heart.' Around nine o'clock, he left to go home.

"New Year's Day was a stormy one. What a gale! The wind blew from the northeast, and it blew for three days. Well, it finally cleared up and we spent the day shovelling out. We wondered about Nicky, knowing that by now all of the family's food would be gone. The following day, around two o'clock, Bill White—he lived next door to Nicky—came

49

down here in a hurry, and when he came through that door I knew there was something wrong. He had a funny colour. He said, 'Silas, I think there's something gone awfully wrong up at Nicky's.'

"'Why?' I asked.

"'Well, just before dinner, we saw Nicky and Annie go out into the woodshed and shut the door behind them. A few minutes later, Nicky came out and tied the door behind him. After ten minutes passed, we saw him go out into the woodshed with two of his girls. That was all we thought about it. But just now we heard a gunshot and it came from inside Nicky's house! We waited for a few minutes but no one came out. There's nothing stirring around the house and the woodshed door is still tied shut.'

"'My blessed God,' I said. 'Go around the harbour and get some men!'

"Bill left and I put on my clothes and took two of my sons and went up to Nicky's. My heart almost failed as I neared his house. I'll never forget it, Doctor. When I opened the door to the kitchen, there it was."

Dr. Grenfell told this story on the BBC in 1908. "Things were so desperate along the Labrador coast in 1892 when I first landed there, that one man, rather than see his family starve, killed his wife and family with an axe, then shot himself." He told this story many times afterwards, saying that of all the things he heard in his lifetime, this was the saddest.

"Doctor," said Silas, "Nicky was on the floor near the table with a hole in his chest—he'd shot himself. And near him was his oldest daughter. She'd been killed with an axe, the axe that was near him. The men started to arrive, and the next thing I knew my mind went completely blank.

"The men went out into the woodshed and discovered Annie and the two youngest children—Nicky had killed the three of them with the axe. They found the oldest boy, too, in the bedroom. He'd also been killed with the axe. Two of the men there haven't gotten over it yet, and I don't expect they ever will.

"Doctor, if the fish merchants would only let us have just a little food! Without mercy, they walked away from our women and children and left them to starve."

Dr. Grenfell had been undergoing a transformation throughout Silas's story. Now he dropped his face into his hands and wept openly. A few minutes later, he regained his composure and looked at this leather-faced Labradorian through his tears. His voice was hoarse with emotion. "Did you report this to the authorities, Silas?"

"No," said Silas, "it's no use. The government is made up of fish merchants, or it's fish merchants who control the government. It'll never change. We don't have anyone to turn to."

Grenfell shook his head in disbelief. "Something has to be done, Silas. I'm going to do something about it."

Silas gasped. "You are?"

"Yes, I am."

Grenfell made ready to check on his young patient again, but a thought struck him. He looked at Silas curiously. "Do you have a dental problem?" he asked.

Silas looked at the doctor as if not knowing what he meant. Grenfell reworded his question.

"Do you have trouble with your teeth?"

The old man grunted. "I've been crazy now with a toothache for a month."

"Let me have a look."

Silas opened his mouth, and what he saw made Wilfred Thomason Grenfell, M.D. devote his entire life to the medical needs of Labrador and northern Newfoundland.

SIX

Jack jumped from the rail of the schooner and landed in the centre of the little rowboat. It rocked under his weight as he put the oars out and started rowing toward shore. He looked back at the schooner, feeling weak and shaken after what had just happened. Molly wasn't on deck. She hadn't come up out of the forecastle to wave or call to him like she had always done before.

Jack was in shock. He had disobeyed his father, and how! What if he were questioned? They would have to lie, both he and Molly. *But I'm a man now, and Molly is a woman.* Striking the shore, Jack leaped out onto the rocks and hitched the boat to a boulder. He walked over to the lumber and started working.

Molly stood near the table in the forecastle, trying to wash the dishes. Tears ran down her face. "What have I done? Mother! Oh, Mother!" she cried. "It's all my fault, because I was the one who tempted Jack." She brushed away her tears and said, "I'm not sure what I've done, but I know that I've done wrong."

She had never been told the facts of life. The only thing she had been told was to stay away from men and boys until she was ready to get married. Instinctively, she knew that what she and Jack had done was contrary to what was expected of her. She had been told fervently that if a girl found herself in what they called the family way before she was married and something happened whereby she didn't get married, she would be doomed for the rest of her life. In other words, the sinful girl carried a black mark forever. Molly was frightened, certain that she would suffer for having committed this sin.

She again heard the reproachful words of Skipper Joe. *Don't allow anyone into the galley, Molly.* But she had! She had allowed Jack—her Jack—into the galley.

All of a sudden, Molly had an idea. Perhaps the skipper would marry them if they asked. He was a lay reader with the Methodist Church, and she had attended marriage ceremonies performed by him back home.

Taking a deep breath, she said, "Yes, we'll get the skipper to marry us." Her spirits lifted, and her tears quickly dried up.

Smiling, Molly headed for the upper deck and into the sunlight. Her smile widened as she said, "I think I'll call out to Jack and see if he still loves me."

Two days after leaving Snug Harbour, two full days of battling ice, the *Albert* arrived at a place called Domino, Labrador. There were a lot of schooners there, and of course plenty of sick people. Dr. Grenfell said that this was the place where his medical work in Labrador really began, the place where most Labrador schooners congregated at some point or another on their way to or from the Labrador fishery, which was the largest of its kind in the world.

On arriving in Domino, Grenfell introduced himself as a medical doctor and posted a letter on a wall, a writ that gave him the authority to practice medicine in Labrador. He soon had a large lineup of people seeking medical attention.

Late that evening, after the rush of visitors to the clinic was over, the young doctor came on deck and stood near the railing, looking out at the small houses onshore. Deep in thought, he espied a small boat, and upon closer inspection he saw that it was merely a bunch of boards nailed together with dabs of tar along the seams. It moved toward him at a steady rate, until at about a hundred feet from him it stopped. In the boat, sitting very still and quiet, was a young boy, his face bronze and his hair brown. He was wearing clothes that were much too big for him.

The boy sat with the oars in his hands, staring fixedly at the doctor. Grenfell held up his hand in a friendly gesture, and after some hesitation the boy pushed the small craft closer to him. Cupping his mouth with his hand, he asked, "Do you be a real doctor?"

"That is what they call me."

"Us hasn't got any m-m-money at all," the boy stammered, "but there's a dying man ashore, and I come to ask ye if youse could come and take a look at him."

"Come a little closer, young man," said Grenfell. The look of this young man, malnourished, skittish and filthy, was one of desperation. "Yes, I certainly will," he said upon closer inspection.

Grenfell summoned Harry Taylor, and once ashore, the boy escorted them to a sod-covered house. The doctor was dismayed at the state of these living quarters. He said that this house made all the Irish huts he had seen before look like mansions. The floor was merely beach rocks spread among black mud, the windows were holes covered with pieces of broken glass, and the walls were made of earth. It was just a hole dug in an embankment, with a wooden front and roof.

A small stove sat in the corner, with an iron stovepipe going up through a hole in the roof. Bunks along the wall were arranged in tiers, and the six children in them looked neglected and frightened. As the men entered, the children huddled together in a corner, and in one of the lower bunks, in near darkness, they saw a very sick man, coughing his heart out. A frail woman dressed in rags sat near him, feeding him cold water with a spoon.

Silence fell on the room as Grenfell knelt to examine the man. He had a rampant high fever and a bad case of pneumonia, and it appeared that he also had tuberculosis. Grenfell surveyed the room, and his heart sank. This was no place for a sick man. He first thought of taking the man aboard the *Albert* and admitting him to their small hospital ward there, but to sail away with this man on board, who was now dying, and who was a husband and father...

The young doctor's heart ached as he stared at this family. Suppose the patient died three or four days after they left Domino, when they would be a hundred miles farther up the northern coast—who would claim the body? They would have to bury him at sea, or in an unmarked grave somewhere in an unnamed cove along the Labrador coast. Sailing away with this father and husband and not bringing him back again was unthinkable. If only there were a hospital where he could take him. What could he do? He cleaned the sick man and gave the family advice, medicine, and packages of food. What shook Grenfell up most was the knowledge that this family was near starvation, with no one to provide for them. He gathered the family around him and prayed. He wished them God's blessing and said goodbye.

Dr. Grenfell recorded that a couple of months later, as the cool weather returned, he was heading south and came into Domino again. He went ashore and paid a visit to this sod hut again, only to find that the family's situation had worsened; the family of six was headed by a widow, as he expected. The man had passed on, leaving his wife and family destitute, except for the bit of government dole of twenty dollars a year, a meagre allowance that had to be taken up in food at a floating fish merchant's store. Grenfell swore he would establish a place on the Labrador to care for the sick and destitute.

The cold winds that blow in from the Labrador Sea, even in June and July, sometimes pierce the toughest of men to the bone if they're not properly dressed, and often they're caught unawares. The fishing crews that went to the Labrador in the 1890s and around the turn of the century weren't interested in any kind of a suntan or a romp at midnight on some sandy beach. No, when they went aboard their fishing boats a little before dawn and picked up their oars to row to the fishing grounds, they were dressed for the chilly morning air. Their ruddy complexions quickly turned leathery as these young boys took the place of men, some only thirteen years of age, and it didn't take them long to learn what it took to keep out the cold, damp moisture that would drip from their faces as they moved and tossed through the early morning fog.

On this cold morning, Skipper Joe Budden directed his crew, who were pulling on the oars just a few feet from the cliffs. There was no engine noise, and no music being played to distract this old sea dog from the finer points of navigating his wooden basket. The ocean breakers slammed against the cliffs nearby and rolled back again to the mighty deep.

As the men rowed, only the skipper spoke. "I'd say that this is one morning she's right full to the corks with fish. You can almost smell them." The old man smiled, baring his scattered teeth. Even in these conditions, the thought of having the trap full of fish made him happy. No one commented; they continued pulling hard on the oars.

Due to the favourable high tides, the previous evening they had put the schooner ashore and fixed the rudder casing. "Thank God," Skipper Joe had said, "she's not leaking anymore." Today they would be moving into the tarpaper shack they had built on the shore. It would be a pleasure to be able to lie down without rolling in their bunks. They had also constructed a small wharf with a stagehead, just a few small logs nailed together with rocks packed on top of them. It would serve as a temporary landing to avoid having to climb over the slippery rocks. Everything except the cooking gear and sleeping equipment was put ashore. The coarse fishing salt was left on board, because it was to be used in curing the fish on the schooner.

Jack was fearless. When setting a trap, it took a good nerve to be the shore person when the sea was rough, and people who have never seen or been involved in the cod trap fishery in Newfoundland cannot possibly know what it entails. When anchoring a cod trap anywhere in the ocean, it is also attached to the land nearby. In order to do this on a mountainous shore, someone has to drive a steel spike into a crevice in the cliffside, and it has to be anchored firmly enough to keep a trap full of fish from being tugged away by the Arctic current sweeping alongshore.

A special man is needed, someone who understands what it's all about. First, he has to be confident, never fearing the huge waves that roll in. He also has to be able to move with catlike agility along the slippery rocks. Finally, he has to be able to use a ten-pound hammer to drive a steel spike into the cliff. Jack was the man.

On this morning, Jack was needed at the cod trap, and for this reason the skipper told Gid to stay back and help Molly move the balance of the supplies from the schooner to the shack.

Molly wasn't afraid of much, but she didn't like the idea of being alone on the Labrador shore. She had heard so much about wolves and bears, especially the water bears—polar bears—that it made her nervous just to look at the shoreline. She wanted someone to be around, hoping of course that it would be Jack. The skipper couldn't spare him, but promised that for the first few days, or perhaps for the first week, he would have someone else working there. There was a lot of work to do on land anyway, so she would be busy in the shack and would gradually get used to being alone when all the crew were away.

Three or four days had passed since Molly and Jack's intimate encounter, and by now the impact of their first experience was beginning to wear off. She was madly in love and longed to be with Jack again, but the presence of all the people on the little schooner wouldn't allow them any privacy. Jack had been at the fish continually from early morning 'til late at night for the last three days, but it was obvious to the skipper and the crew that they would have to move ashore soon. Molly looked forward to it. This morning, however, with the fog lifting and the sun beginning to cast its rays around the little cove, the fishing crew was out on the water, and Gid and Molly found themselves alone on the deck of the little schooner.

They quietly worked away, loading the small rowboat with housekeeping items for the shack onshore. "Don't overload the boat, Gid, my son," said Molly.

"No," he said, "I'll take as much as I can get aboard. I thought I might be able to take it all in three trips."

"I'm going ashore with you, Gid, so don't overload her."

"Okay, but you"ll have to get on board."

Molly looked down at him from the deck of the schooner. "You'll have to help me down."

"Okay," he said, as he reached up for her.

"Be careful, Gid, don't let me fall."

"I won't let you fall, Molly, don't worry."

Gid was a likeable fellow, full of wit and humour. He had also grown up with Molly and seen her almost every day when he was home, and their families were very close. Gid put his arms around her slim waist and lifted her down. "Hold on to me tight," he said, "or you'll lose your balance and fall overboard."

Molly firmly held onto him, and Gid was surprised that she didn't pull away when she stepped down in the boat; in fact, she kind of hugged him. They were going to the shack, just the two of them. Gid was a fox, and he knew his chance would come. Molly was young and inexperienced, away from home and afraid. The other men were out to the cod trap, and he was carrying the beds ashore, of all things. Gid felt the blood in his veins rush and his heart pound in his chest. He loosened his hold on Molly, not wanting to frighten her by moving too fast. She would be his for the taking when the time and place were right.

When they reached the stagehead, Gid saw that it would be a hard job for Molly to climb onto the little wharf. "It'll be too hard for you to get up there, Molly. You might fall down, so I'm going to have to put you ashore on the beach. Just hold on."

"You're right, Gid," she said, smiling.

He was thrilled that he'd get his arms around Molly one more time by carrying her ashore. Within a few minutes they neared the rocky shoreline. When the rowboat struck the bottom, Gid stepped out, his long rubber boots pulled up to his thighs. "This punt needs more water than the schooner to float in," he said, as he struggled to pull it closer to the shore. "Okay, darling," he said, his eyes twinkling.

Molly didn't say anything as she stood on the gunwale of the small boat and climbed up on Gid's shoulders from behind, holding his hands tightly. "The rocks are slippery, so wait 'til I help you up over them," he said. "You could break your neck with what you have on your feet."

She agreed. Gid caught her hand and led her to safe footing.

"Thanks, Gid," Molly said.

"Let's get this stuff out as quick as we can. I'll go out and get another load. You can start bringing this up to the cabin." In an hour they had all the things that were needed for the cabin brought ashore and carried up.

"I'm tired, Gid. Let's rest for a few minutes," Molly said as they approached the cabin on the last trip. "Let's go inside; at least we'll be in the shade."

The sun was shining and hot as it lifted its scorching face over the eastern horizon and peeked around the little cove, spotting Gid and Molly. It knew what they had on their minds, and it drove them indoors among the feather beds and away from any watchful eyes.

There was only one room partitioned off in the cabin, and this was reserved for Molly. The skipper wanted to give her some privacy, a place where she could wash or undress without anyone seeing her. He had built a bunk out of boards, a place to lay out her feather mattress; this would make a comfortable bed. In her room, Molly had a double-paned window, permitting a clear view of the cove, the schooner, and anyone who approached from the water.

The cabin was made of rough lumber and covered outside with tarpaper, or what is called single-ply felt. It was held in place by strips tacked on about two feet apart. This prevented the wind from blowing through the seams. Inside there was a homemade stove, built in such a way that it had a large oven on top of the stove deck and the firebox beneath the oven, a practical arrangement for baking.

"Let's go in on your bunk and rest for a few minutes, Molly," Gid said in a joking manner, but resting was the furthest thing from his mind.

Molly said, "No, we can't, because the skipper might come and catch us. You know what he said. No one is supposed to come handy to me."

"I'm handy to you now, Molly, and the skipper will never know it." He put his arms around her and kissed her, and she didn't resist. The shame she had felt after her encounter with Jack a few days earlier was quickly forgotten.

Gid kissed her again, and before the two of them knew it they were across Molly's bed, while the skipper and his crew, including Jack, continued hauling their cod trap, somewhere far out on the ocean.

SEVEN

It was close to the end of August when the *Albert* sailed into Mugford Tickle, Labrador. In writing about it years later, Dr. Grenfell said that his first year on the Labrador wasn't only a medical mission of mercy, but also a survey of needs that helped him put together a long-term plan for the well-being of the people. As he entered the small harbour of Mugford Tickle, he was appalled at the desperation and the total isolation he saw there. The small shacks scattered around the shoreline were propped up on sticks that could barely hold their weight, and sod huts were built up against the base of the little hills just back from the shoreline. Smoke climbed weakly out of their pipes.

"It looks like there are people living underground in there, Captain," said Grenfell.

Captain Trezise could only shake his head in amazement.

Moored in the harbour was a very large schooner. They learned that it was owned by a floating merchant that came in the spring and brought supplies to fishermen along the coast, staying until it took on a full load of fish for transport to the outside. This large vessel had a crew who fished also. They operated under the truck system: the merchant would advance supplies in exchange for salted fish, and if the fishermen in

61

Mugford Tickle did poorly with the fish, the large vessel would work its way back along the coast, collecting fish and giving out supplies to people they could depend on. This ensured that the livyers were dependent on them. Grenfell saw the danger inherent in this arrangement. With no predetermined value on the goods advanced or on the cod to be used as payment, this system was open to widespread abuse by the merchants.

After the *Albert* dropped anchor and settled in, a few people came aboard, the inquisitive ones, and learned that there was a doctor aboard doing free medical work along the coast. As Dr. Grenfell and Captain Trezise stood on deck looking at the meagre surroundings, they saw a small rowboat leave the large schooner and come toward them. Two men were in the boat, one rowing while the other stood and kept his eyes on the *Albert*. When they pulled up to the side, they remained silent.

"Good day, men," said Grenfell.

"Good day," they replied in kind. They threw the painter to the *Albert's* crew, and Captain Trezise caught it. The man who was standing asked, "Do ye have a doctor on board, sir?"

"Yes, we do. I am the doctor, sir," said Grenfell. "Come aboard."

"We have no time to come aboard, Doctor. We're putting away fish. Our captain sent us over to ask if you'd come over and have a look at one of the girls. She's sick and the captain thinks she's going to die."

The man ended his sentence quickly, nervously, as if to say *I delivered the message, and that's it.*

Grenfell was surprised to learn that a female was aboard such a vessel, so far beyond the usual fishing grounds of summer crews. "Yes, we'll be right over," he replied.

The crew of the *Albert* launched a boat and took the doctor and his assistant to the schooner. When they boarded the Newfoundland vessel, the crew stopped their fishing activities as the visitors were introduced to their captain.

The captain took the doctor to one side and had a talk with him. "I know what's the matter with Pearl," he said as he looked at Grenfell. "She got herself in the family way. I 'lows she was like it before she left home, that is, before she came on board with us.

"I asked her if she was, and she said she wasn't, but we all know what went on. One of the men was even found in the bunk with her!"

Grenfell looked at the captain. "Are you telling me that the girl is pregnant?"

The captain looked worried. "She was, but according to Rosy she isn't now."

"What happened?"

"Well, Doctor, Rosy said that she had a three-month-old baby."

"Who is Rosy, Skipper?"

"Rosy is the other serving girl. She said that Pearl took sick one night and had the baby. That's all I know about it."

Grenfell replied, "This girl must have had a premature birth. Is that what you're saying?"

"I suppose that's what you call it, Doctor."

"Did you say that she is in the forecastle?"

"Yes, in one of the bunks. She's been there now for three days."

The young doctor walked up to the darkened corner of the forecastle.

"Can you please get me another light of some kind, Captain?"

"Yes, sir." The captain dashed away and came back in seconds with a brightly burning lantern.

To see the captain so eager to help pleased Grenfell immensely. He took the light to the poor girl, and after a thorough examination he found her to be in a terrible state, but not incurable. Pearl had given birth to a child, however. He would have to talk to her and Rosy, the girl whom he suspected had helped with the delivery.

Grenfell asked the captain if he could leave him alone with the girls for a private conversation. Rosy said that Pearl was fifteen years old, and confirmed that she had delivered a premature baby. Rosy, Pearl's assistant, was only sixteen years old herself, and as ignorant about child-bearing as a ten-year-old boy. And now this fifteen-year-old mother lay in her bunk, untouched, absolutely filthy and helpless, crying and wanting to die. She had been there for over three days in this horrid condition.

He talked softly and informed Pearl that she could be cured, but that he would have to take her off the schooner. Before leaving St. John's, Grenfell had sent a letter of introduction to the Moravian Missions along the Labrador coast, informing them of his medical assistance and requesting any support they could provide. When put to the test they did provide medical aid, and in this case he knew he could depend on them to help with this needy patient. From Mugford Tickle he could safely transport Pearl to the Moravian Mission Station at Okak without losing her.

"We're going to take you on our hospital ship where we can look after you."

Grenfell could hardly believe that she was no more than a child, just fifteen years of age. She looked frightened, even wild, and she pleaded with her friend. "Rosy, tell him that I'm not going. Tell him that I want to die. Rosy, will you tell the doctor why I want to die?"

Grenfell motioned for Rosy to join him near the stove. When they both crowded into the small space, he asked her to explain the girl's behaviour. "Why would she say she wants to die?"

"Doctor," Rosy said with unease, "she's frightened that her people back home are going to find out that she had a baby. It doesn't matter if it lived or died. Her people will disown her for the rest of her life, and she'll be an outcast."

"Why?" Grenfell asked, shocked.

"Because they are religious, sir."

"What? Can't they find forgiveness in their hearts?"

"That's the way it is, Doctor. If you do something like that, you'll be condemned forever."

Rosy started to cry. She was a beautiful girl, but she was already scarred and aged by hard work and worry. Grenfell sighed. "Where are the remains of the birth?"

"One of the men wrapped it in a blanket and went ashore and buried it, Doctor."

Well, he thought, *at least the child had a burial.*

Grenfell sensed that Rosy was scared, but he pressed for more information. "Rosy, do you know who the father of the child was?" When she didn't answer, he rephrased the question. "Let me ask you this. Do you know if one of the men on board here is the father of the child?"

Rosy sniffed. "No, sir. She was in the family way before she came aboard the schooner. I was the only one who knew she was going to have a baby, from that time until it was born."

Grenfell reassured Rosy that Pearl would be all right. "Can you tell her that she shouldn't be thinking this way? She has to go on with her life. We will make her better."

He went back to the forecastle and proceeded to clean up the frightened girl and get her ready to be transferred to the hospital ship. He recorded all the necessary information he could gather concerning her from Rosy, and later from the captain, who was eager to help.

The captain gave Grenfell a sum of money to pay for the costs. He was fraught with concern for Pearl. "I have a daughter of my own, Doctor, back home. If you can, I'd like you to help change her attitude."

Grenfell knew what he meant. When the captain left, the sick girl cried out. "I don't want to go, Doctor. I just want to stay here and die."

The young doctor held her hand and said, "I will take you to wonderful people who will love and take care of you and make you better."

Still, Pearl pleaded to be left alone to die. The doctor ignored her while he wrapped her in blankets and prepared to take her off the schooner. The crew carried her up onto the deck while he dictated a note to his assistant. This was to be delivered to Captain Trezise, advising him of what had transpired and requesting that he pull the *Albert* up alongside the large schooner to transfer the patient.

The *Albert* left Mugford Tickle and headed for the Moravian Mission station at Okak. Two years later, in 1903, Grenfell would open a hospital there and staff it with a full-time resident doctor, S. K. Hutton.

Dr. Grenfell, in telling the story years later, said that this was an event that he never did forget—it haunted him. The Moravian Missionary's wife was a nurse who gave Pearl the best treatment and care that could be given, but to no avail. The young girl moaned and cried day and night, pleading for death to take away the shame.

Unendingly she begged, "I want to die, I want to die. Don't make me go home again. I can't go home again, I just want to die."

His notes recorded that Pearl had gotten much better physically and was on the mend, but also that she was frightened at the thought of what would happen to her when and if her family found out about her pregnancy.

She simply willed herself to die. In spite of all the care and love that was given her at the Moravian Mission Station, Pearl collapsed and died a few days after arriving.

Grenfell wrote that it must have been a pitiful sight, the small boat bearing the remains of this young girl wrapped in the flag of her native Newfoundland, rowing to a rocky headland for interment. Everyone cried as they removed the flag from the coffin and piled rocks on the shallow grave that held the remains of this poor girl. There she lay, resting in the frozen ground of Labrador until that great eternal day.

A few years later, Dr. Grenfell was working his way north when he passed the same headland. He was moved so much by the fate of this young woman that he decided to visit her grave. As he walked up to the pile of rocks that protected her bleached bones, he read aloud the words on the wooden cross that he had ordered to be erected on her grave. The words were still clear for all to see: NEITHER DO I CONDEMN THEE.

EIGHT

The schooner was only one-third loaded with fish when the trap fishery came to an end that summer. For a full week now, whenever they hauled the trap, they had a water haul, meaning "not a fish."

"We'll have no choice but to take the traps out of the water and put the trawls out," Skipper Joe said as they ate lunch. "We'll also go fishing with hook-and-line. Maybe the fish have moved out into deeper water. I've seen this happen before."

"I don't think so, not this early," said Roy.

"Well, what do you think is happening?"

"I think the fish we caught were part of a school that came to the land and was moving south. For one thing, the caplin haven't been here yet, and they're guaranteed to come. Then there'll be fish, and lots of them."

The skipper wasn't so sure. "We can't take a chance, Roy, because September is right around the corner, you know."

"Father, it's only August. We still have a chance with the traps."

Skipper Joe looked worried. "We can't afford to wait, so we might as well start getting the trawls ready this afternoon."

The rest of the crew agreed. Fish was what they wanted, and they wouldn't get any by staying onshore.

Molly awoke in the middle of the night. She didn't feel well. A weakness came over her, and a flush lit her face. During the last two days she had been having cramps in her stomach, and for the second month in a row she had missed her period. Now, as she lay in her small bed in the darkness of the night with her face to the wall of the tarpaper shack, she asked herself a question. "Am I going to have a baby?"

The thought frightened her, and she quickly sat up. Dizziness overtook her. This was the first time in her life she had ever experienced this kind of feeling. Something had to be wrong. "No, I'm not, I know I'm not pregnant," she whispered in denial as she lay back on her bed and pulled the blankets up over her head.

I have had Jack, and oh how I love him. A voice pierced the silence of her heart. *Molly, what about Gid? Do you love Gid, Molly? It could be him.*

She lay still, and all of a sudden she began to sob. Her pale cheeks glistened, and the tears she cried made her long dark hair fall unnoticed, matted and limp. Whatever she did, she mustn't be heard crying, especially here, because the skipper heard every sound that was made in the cabin. But surely this kind old man would never let anything happen to her, no matter what she had done. The chance that he might accept what had happened lifted her spirits for a moment, and she stopped crying. In an hour, the men would be getting ready to go out fishing again. She closed her eyes and drifted off to sleep.

The trap fishery was all but over along the Labrador coast for the season, and it looked as if it would be a hard struggle for Skipper Joe Budden and his six-man crew to get a fair voyage this summer. It was one of those summers when the codfish came early but only stayed near the shores for a short time before leaving. They said that the caplin spawned in deep water. A few had come to shore, but not like other years, and they only stayed a few days. So, when they went, the hungry cod chased them. The skipper and his crew had gone out on the fishing grounds and found a good sign of fish off there. However, this fish had to be caught by trawls and hook-and-line, and August found them throwing baited hooks and lines over the gunwales.

During this period, around the turn of the century, a captain on a small vessel was lucky to have a compass, let alone any instrument to tell the weather. There was no radio of any kind, and it was only the well-to-do and the most successful fishing skippers who had a weather glass, but they were all very well trained in telling the weather by watching the sky for signs of approaching storms. Although they were fairly accurate most of the time, it was the unexpected and the unforeseen that took its toll. More than anything else, it was worry that caused the faces of Newfoundlanders and Labradorians to be drawn and wrinkled at an early age.

Most of the schooners and small boats were made from softwood, held together with square iron nails. Many proved to be no match for the fury of an angry ocean hungry for the bones of any man, woman or child who dared make a misjudgment.

This was the situation Skipper Joe Budden and his crew found themselves in the summer of 1892. After the fifteenth of August, it was clear to them that they wouldn't be leaving the Labrador until the last of September at the earliest, that is, if they were to get a full load of salted cod. By then, the stormy season would be upon them. To leave with just part of a load of fish meant there would be a shortage of money earned, leaving bills unpaid and less food for the winter. Worst of all, it would result in very angry merchants, and for those reasons Skipper Joe was forced to stay and fish, even if it meant staying on the Labrador coast until Christmas. He had heard talk of this happening to fishermen before, but never to him. Almost every day now he saw the sails of schooners heading south, undoubtedly carrying loads of fish. They were the ones who had good fishing and caught as much as they could carry.

One evening, around mid-September, Skipper Joe and his crew stood aboard the schooner, processing their day's catch of cod, six barrels in total. They had done very well with their trawls and handlines and were working hard in the late afternoon sun with nothing else to disturb them, when someone spotted a large schooner pushing its way into the small harbour.

"Look, coming in there, boys." The speaker pointed in the direction of the harbour's entrance. Everyone stopped and stared. The schooner was what they called a "banker." Anyone who knew anything about ships could tell it was the type that fished offshore. It was a large schooner, with high stacks of dories on deck.

They spotted a large number of men on deck tying down the canvas and getting ready to let the anchors go. As the large schooner came nearer, the Budden crew heard a dog barking.

"Sounds like they have a team of dogs aboard, Father," Roy said.

Skipper Joe said, "At least one."

Everyone admired the great skill with which this large vessel was being manoeuvred around the little harbour. Once the anchors were in place and the vessel's head pointed toward the harbour entrance, her stern was no more than a hundred feet from Skipper Joe's own little schooner. They were now in hailing distance.

"I'd say the skipper on that one knows what he's doing," Roy said.

"I'd say so too," the skipper replied.

Within half an hour, the banker's crew had everything tidied away and all the rope coiled in place. The men were now positioned along the stern rails, looking at Skipper Joe and his crew. Some of them saw that there was a woman with his crew, helping with the fish, and they began to whistle at her. Molly stopped her work and looked at them and smiled. She read aloud the white lettering on the back of the vessel. "LUNENBURG, N. S."

"I didn't think she was from Newfoundland. That stands for Nova Scotia," Bill stated. They watched as the crew lowered a boat. "I think they're coming ashore," he added.

"Maybe so," the skipper said. Within a few minutes two men were down in the boat with four oarsmen. They came directly to Skipper Joe's little schooner.

"Are we permitted to come aboard, sir?" asked the man standing in the middle of the boat.

The skipper greeted them. "Why, yes, by all means. We'd love to have you aboard."

The man stepped in over the rail. "Good evening, gentlemen," he said. He looked at Molly. "And you too, miss. It looks like you have had some luck with the fish today."

"A little," said Skipper Joe.

The stranger continued. "We were moored in this cove a couple of years ago when we ran in to get shelter from a storm. We were caught for a solid week, but we were all right. Like a bug in a rug, as they say."

He continued in a sad voice, his eyes fastened on the deck in front of his feet. "But this time we've come in here for a different reason. We've come to bury two of our men."

Skipper Joe said, "I'm sorry to hear that, sir. It won't be a very easy task."

"I'm the captain of our vessel, Charlie Edwards, out of Nova Scotia, and I've been fishing offshore now for over two months. About a week ago we saw a steamer heading straight for us. When she got near us she hove to and we learned her name was the *Harmony*. The captain told us that he had just dropped off freight at a Moravian Mission somewhere on the Labrador, in a place called Okak. He had extra supplies on board and asked us if we needed some, since they were headed to St. John's to pick up a load of dried cod to take overseas. Of course, we accepted."

Captain Edwards had a sudden fit of coughing. When it passed, he said, "I sent two of my men aboard the ship to accept the supplies and pay for them, and so they did, and away she went. The following day the two men took violently ill, so fast it was apparent within hours that they were in a serious condition. I suspected they were fatally ill, and I was proven right when they lasted only a couple of days. The way those two died, I guarantee you they both had typhoid fever. I've seen it before, and it was just like what they had. The captain on the German ship told my two men when they went on board that they weren't supposed to go wandering around the ship, because some of the crew were sick. He also said that there was a young English doctor going around Labrador giving medical aid to the people, and that he'd given the *Harmony's* officers medicine for the crew. They said that his name was Grenfell."

He let out another series of harsh coughs. "It was too late for us to go look for this Dr. Grenfell because they died so quickly, but before they did they made one last request: they didn't want to be buried at sea. I gave them my word, and this is why we're in here today."

Skipper Joe could see that this fellow was made of cast iron, but also that this ordeal had shaken him up. "One of the men pleaded with tears in his eyes just before he died. 'Oh, Captain,' he said, 'don't bury us at sea. Make sure you bury us in the ground.'"

The old man was himself concerned after hearing this sad tale. "I'm very sorry to hear this, Captain, and our hearts go out to you and your crew. We'll assist you in the burial of your two comrades if you so request, and we'll lend a hand if we can help in any other way."

"That's very kind of you, sir," Edwards replied before coughing again. "I'm not much of a hand at burying the dead on the land, Captain Budden. On the sea I know what to do, but on the shore? That's a different matter.

"You see, I suppose a Bible is needed on the land, and that's one thing we don't have."

Skipper Joe nodded. "I have a Bible and a prayer book and a minister's manual. The burial rite is in it, but that's not a problem anyway, because I know it from memory. I'll go and get them for you right away, for whenever you need it."

Captain Edwards looked relieved. "Sir, could I ask you to do us one more favour?"

"If I can, sure."

"Will you take over and bury my two men?"

"Yes, sir, I will. All you have to do is let me know when you want it done."

Edwards was anxious. "This evening if it's possible, so that we can move on and not lose any time."

Skipper Joe looked at the fish strewn around the deck. "We should have our fish put away in about an hour or so, and then we'll be ready."

"Don't worry about your fish, Captain—what was your name again, sir?"

"Joe Budden."

"Okay, Captain Budden. I'll put a group of my men here in your place to help with the fish. You can go and get the things ready for the burial."

The skipper charged Bill with the responsibility of overseeing the putting away of their fish, and informed their visitors that the first thing they should do is pick out a suitable place to dig the graves.

"You're right," Captain Edwards said. "I'll have my men come right away and do that."

Skipper Joe and Molly left for the cabin onshore, and when they were out of earshot, the Nova Scotian captain asked Bill, "What is he, a clergy?"

"He's a part-time lay reader with the Methodist Church in the winter, when he's home," Bill replied.

Roy grinned and said, "And full-time in the summer when he can get anyone to listen to him."

Bill gave Roy a look that said *Shut up*.

Captain Edwards said, "I thought so, because he seems different from all the rest."

He cupped his hands around his mouth and called out in a rough voice, "Hey, David!"

A man appeared by the railing and shouted across to the smaller schooner. "Yes, Captain Edwards?"

"Send over seven or eight men with their oilclothes to help these men put away their fish, and another five or six with shovels to dig the graves."

"Right away, Skipper."

"And David, there's no need for everyone to go at that, so have some of the men take four water barrels and fill them onshore."

All the men were on the move and the little cove was buzzing with activity. A boat from the large banker landed a group of men on one side of Skipper Joe's schooner, and they set about at once to help put away the fish. They were professional fishermen, fitted to go to work with rubber clothes and gloves, some with knives. A group carrying shovels landed at the wharf while the water detail landed at the brook, farther out in the harbour.

Molly had gone ashore with Skipper Joe to help him get ready for the burial, but before they left the skipper told Bill to assist the Nova Scotian men in locating a gravesite. "Go up along those short trees if it's possible. You might find a place up there to bury those two poor souls." They selected a site overlooking the harbour not too far from their cabin, and the men began digging the graves, side by side.

In half an hour, Skipper Joe was transformed from grubby fisherman to clean-cut clergyman. He had washed and shaved and put on a three-piece suit. Although it was baggy around the knees and elbows, no one paid any heed when he appeared among the rocky cliffs and the grassy knolls. He looked resplendent, and they all stared in disbelief. After he was assured that everything was going fine, he re-entered the cabin and sat down at the table. He opened his prayer book and minister's manual and read the section that outlined the procedures for burial services.

Molly had also adorned herself in her Sunday best, a dress she had carefully packed before leaving home. She tidied up the cabin and prepared a lunch for the Nova Scotian captain, who would be invited for a cup of tea after the funeral.

As he meditated on the short message he would deliver at the gravesite, Skipper Joe said to Molly, "My dear, would it be possible for you to sing a song during the service for the two men? A song would add so much, and might lift the spirits of everyone who attended. It would be wonderful if you could." He knew that Molly could sing very well, because he had heard her sing many times back home during regular church meetings and at special events.

Molly wasn't happy at the thought of singing when she thought about the strangers who would be there, but more so because she hadn't been feeling well these past two days. She hadn't told anyone that she was barely able to keep up, almost staggering with pain, and she continued to work hard. She hadn't had a period for over two months, and the thought of being pregnant frightened her.

Night after night she had lain awake, worrying over the fact that she could be in the family way, although Jack had promised to marry her. She was still worried that the skipper would find out, though he would surely protect her in some way. Her family and the people back home were a different matter.

Gathering her thoughts—*Oh, yes, the skipper's request*— she said, "Yes, sir, but only if you can get Fred to accompany me on his mouth organ."

"I don't think that'll be a problem. I'll ask him."

"Okay," Molly said, "I'll decide on a song."

Skipper Joe summoned Fred to the cabin and told him what he had planned. Fred wasn't a shy fellow when it came to music, since he was a regular musician in the church back home, and he immediately agreed to accompany Molly while she sang. He asked her what she intended to sing at the service, and she told him "Amazing Grace," the old familiar standard.

It didn't take long for the Nova Scotian crew to dig two shallow graves among the rocks near the shore and for the others to put away the fish with all the extra help. The mess was cleaned away, and everyone made ready to go to the funeral. Captain Edwards called for the crew to bring the two coffins and ordered everyone else ashore for the funeral. The coffins were made of boards taken from the dories that the two men had fished in.

The coffins were placed on hand barrows and everyone stood in place, ready to move to the gravesite. Skipper Joe emerged from the cabin accompanied by Molly, and they walked down to the shoreline to join the procession.

"Gentlemen, we'll now proceed," the skipper said.

He began to read from the prayer book as the men picked up the coffins and started walking. The younger men had their eyes on Molly as she walked side by side with Captain Edwards, a few steps behind Skipper Joe. The Nova Scotian captain was coughing terribly, and once he had to stop to get his breath.

The men had proven themselves resourceful by finding room to dig two graves among the boulders and cliffs. At the gravesite, the two openings waited to receive their occupants. The pallbearers carefully placed the two boxes on the ground near the gaping holes and stood in silence as Skipper Joe began to read from the Bible. He asked Captain Edwards if there was anything he wanted to say in honour of the two poor men, and after an uncomfortable stretch of coughing, he managed to get out "No, sir, but thank you."

Skipper Joe turned back to the assembled mourners. "We'll now have Molly sing a special song for our two comrades, who wait to go into Mother Earth and to a better world. May God rest their souls. Amen."

"Amen," the crowd repeated.

The skipper nodded to Molly and Fred, cueing them to step forward. Fred took out his harmonica and started to play a few introductory notes, and Molly started to sing. *"Amazing grace, how sweet the sound that saved a wretch like me..."*

The crews of both vessels, young and old, stood around the grave as the sun was going down over the hill, casting a long shadow over the little gathering. It seemed that time stood still for a moment as the sun lingered to catch a glimpse of Molly and hear her sing. She sang naturally from memory, with her face to the sky, her notes in perfect tune with Fred's harmonica. Everyone listened silently as they stood with their caps in hand. They hadn't expected to receive such a rare treat, a beautiful young girl singing sweet music in this barren Labrador cove.

It was a solemn moment for old Captain Edwards.

Skipper Joe began his short message. "We are gathered here on this hillside on this occasion to pay our respects to two departed souls who have gone to reap their reward. As the sun slowly sinks, it lets us know that another day is over and gone. So it is with the life of a man or woman. When the soul has left the body, their time on earth is no more.

"We are about to place the bodies of these two men into the bosom of the great Labrador, which will hold them close until the end of time." The men took the two boxes and lowered them into the graves.

He picked up a handful of sand. "Ashes to ashes and dust to dust. From dust we came and to dust we must return. Amen."

Fred took his harmonica again and started to play as Molly sang, *"There's a land that is fairer than day and by faith, we can see it afar..."*

The two captains and Molly walked to the cabin in the twilight. They went inside, where it was neat and tidy, and although the furniture was all homemade, the cleanliness and the arrangements bore a woman's touch. "Molly, I think the captain would like to have a cup of tea," said Skipper Joe.

"Yes, my dear, I certainly would appreciate one," Captain Edwards said as he sat on a homemade bench near the table. He took out a large red pocket handkerchief and held it to his mouth and started coughing again. When he finished, he said, "I suppose I'll be the next one who'll be going into Mother Earth if this cough doesn't get better. I won't be going into a grave though, because if I die out on the ocean they'll bury me there."

Turning to Molly, he said, "Thank you, my dear, for singing at the service. You'll never know what that meant to all of our crew. And Skipper Joe, you'll never be forgotten."

Captain Edwards took out his wallet and handed the skipper a five-dollar bill.

"I can't take that from you, Captain," Skipper Joe protested, "because what I've done for you this evening was my duty as a minister of the gospel. It's our duty and pleasure to help people, no matter where they come from, whether they're from a foreign country like yours or if they are our own countrymen. It makes no difference. We are all one."

The Nova Scotian captain looked Skipper Joe square in the eye and said, "I'm not giving you this as payment for what you have done. I'm giving you this because you need it, so please, take it."

He placed the money on the table, and although Skipper Joe insisted on not taking it, his argument fell on deaf ears.

The captain fished another five-dollar bill from his pocket and handed it to Molly. She in turn refused payment, but it was no use. Captain Edwards forced her to take it. She looked at the note in awe. It was the first five-dollar bill she had ever seen in her life, let alone owned!

"You people have been so kind to us," he said. "We don't even know how to begin to thank you."

Skipper Joe tried to explain again that it was his duty, but the captain pressed on. "Do you know how difficult the task of burying my two men would have been if you hadn't been here?"

"I'm sure you would have made out fine, but thank you for your kind remarks," said the skipper.

"I only ask you to do one more thing for me, and that is, if you get the time, I want you to put crosses on their graves."

"Yes, we will, and it'll be done tomorrow."

The tea and molasses buns that Molly placed in front of the two men were quickly gobbled up, and the banker captain excused himself for having to leave. He stood up, and the two men shook hands. Captain Edwards put his arms around Molly and gave her a hug and a kiss. "I'll never forget you, my dear. To hear you sing for my crew was a great thing for us all. I'll make sure that the families of the two men hear about it." He turned and walked out the door, the sound of his coughing trailing off in the distance.

An hour later, Molly stood by the cabin window with the five-dollar note in her hand and watched as the banking schooner, with its lights ablaze, picked its way out of the little harbour. The light westerly wind that blew from the Labrador hills bowed the grey canvas, as if preparing the vessel to be blasted off into some unknown world. Tears ran down Molly's face as she recalled the events that had taken place. Standing there, she felt a sudden, terrible pain in the pit of her stomach, and for a moment she thought she was going to faint. As she wiped away her tears she whispered, "There's no doubt I'm in the family way and have been now for three months. What am I going to do? Where can I go? I want Jack to marry me, but if he won't..."

She had to sit down for a minute as the pain gripped her, but just as quickly as it came, it left. She wrapped her hand around the five-dollar bill in her pocket. It was a lot of money, but here in this rock-hole surrounded by the salty ocean, it was next to useless. It could only buy a dream.

PART II

Skipper Joe and Molly

NINE

Skipper Joe Budden finished putting the two crosses on the graves of the Nova Scotian men. He put their names on the markers and covered the graves with rocks. This helped make the crosses very sturdy, capable of standing up against the strong fall winds. Molly hadn't left the cabin today because she wasn't feeling well, and the men had gone to their trawls. They were set on the offshore fishing grounds, where the fish gathered after the caplin and herring became scarce in the inshore waters.

The trawl grounds were approximately six miles from the shoreline, which meant the crew would have to row twelve miles each day—six in the morning, and six back in the evening, hopefully with a full load. How hard the work was depended on the amount of fish and the wind. They would put up their sail if the winds were favourable, and except for really stormy days, this was the normal daily routine.

Skipper Joe would go out with the crew only twice a week, staying ashore most times to make the fish. This process involved washing the surface salt off the fish before spreading it on the flakes or on rocks in the sun to dry. Curing it on the Labrador rather than shipping it home in bulk for making gave it a higher price. Molly normally assisted the skipper when she could, but most of her time was taken up with cooking and cleaning. This she loved and took pride in, but today she wasn't feeling well. She had gotten up early and prepared breakfast for the crew before they left for the fishing banks, but she was feeling so sick that she crawled back in the bunk.

Skipper Joe didn't ask her any questions. She was very pale and quiet this morning; this wasn't like Molly. No matter what time of day it was, she was always a very happy-go-lucky type of person, joking and carrying on, so he thought that she might be tired due to the long season and that a couple of extra hours of sleep would do her good.

Molly had awakened during the night with a terrible pain in her stomach. She could hardly move, and when she managed to stand she had felt faint. As stabs of pain gripped her, she put her hands to her stomach and found that it was unbearably tender, especially in the lower part. Her back also pained. *What's happening to me?* This wasn't a case of diarrhea or the flu. It had to be something worse.

As her senses started to drift away, Molly lowered herself onto the bunk before falling into a dead faint. When she was called at 4:00 A.M., she managed to get out of bed and make breakfast for the men, but it had taken every ounce of strength out of her. When she stood, she felt as if everything inside her would fall out. She was three months pregnant, and although she knew little or nothing about child-bearing or the problems associated with pregnancies, she knew that something was terribly wrong.

The skipper came back to the cabin after erecting the crosses and spreading fish on the flakes. While he was at the fish, he had been thinking about the Nova Scotian captain and the statement he'd made. *I suppose I'll be the next one who'll be going into Mother Earth.*

Was Captain Edwards also sick? Was he coming down with the typhoid fever? That cough of his suggested he was coming down with something. Why did he put his arms around Molly and kiss her? "Molly is sick this morning, the first time since she left home. I wonder..."

He made his way to the cabin, expecting to see Molly with a lunch ready on the table as usual, but the fire had gone out and there was absolute silence.

"Molly. Molly!" he called.

"Yes, Skipper."

"Molly, my dear, where are you? What's wrong?" Skipper Joe said, concern in his voice.

"I'm still in bed, Skipper. I don't feel very well."

"May I come in?"

"Yes, if you like, sir," Molly said.

Skipper Joe went to her makeshift bedroom and pulled back the screen. When he saw her in her bunk, he became worried. She was a picture of death. "What's wrong, Molly, my dear?"

Molly had turned toward the wall, and tears streamed down her face. She had fainted a couple of times, but this was unknown to the skipper. Struggling to face him, she said, "I don't know, Skipper." She had made up her mind that she would never tell anyone what her trouble was, even if she died.

"Where do you feel sick, my dear? Are you getting the flu?"

"I think I am, Skipper. I'm coming down with a sore throat. It's the flu, sir, I know." She closed her eyes as the pain in her back and stomach gripped her.

"I hope you don't get it too bad. I'll get you a cup of tea right away."

"Thank you," she replied, grimacing.

Skipper Joe sat silently in the kitchen as the water heated up. A couple of times he thought he heard Molly groaning in pain. "My, oh my, she must be very sick."

"Molly, do you have a fever, my dear?" he called.

"Yes I think so, Skipper," was the faint reply.

"Do you want me to put a cold cloth on your forehead?"

"No, not now sir," she mumbled.

A thought struck Skipper Joe like a hammer. *Suppose she has typhoid fever? Suppose she caught it from Captain Edwards? That kiss he gave her could be the death of her.* Could it be true? The thought made his heart sink.

The water was boiled, so he went outside and emptied the teapot. He tossed the old tea leaves into a bucket and returned to the cupboard. He put a handful of fresh, loose tea into the pot and poured in the steaming water.

Skipper Joe felt sick himself at the thought that Molly could have typhoid fever. It meant certain death if not treated properly. Sometimes people survived it, like he had years before, but not many did. He also thought about his crew; if Molly had typhoid fever, they were bound to catch it. What could he do? He was sick with worry.

As he made the tea, he called, "Do you want anything to eat, Molly, my dear?"

"No, Skipper, just tea."

Satisfied with her answer, he took the cup of fresh tea to her bunk. He dragged a bench over to her bed. "Do you feel weak, my dear?" Skipper Joe had known Molly since she was born. In fact, he recalled that he had christened her, and before that he'd attended her parents' wedding. Now as he looked at her, he feared the worst. He fought back his tears, because he didn't want her to see him upset.

"Do you have a headache, Molly?"

She spoke but didn't open her eyes. "Yes, Skipper Joe, I'm burning up all over, and my head is splitting."

He said nothing. *It's a sign of typhoid fever, all right.* He pillowed her up and handed her the tea.

"Thank you, Skipper," Molly said and took a few mouthfuls. She was having terrible pains, but she didn't tell him.

"Lie me back, sir, please," she begged.

The skipper removed the pillows and let her lie flat on her back. "How do you feel now, my dear?" he asked.

"I feel pretty good, sir," she lied.

"You'll be all right by tomorrow. You could be right; you may have the flu or something."

"Yes, sir, I hope that's all it is."

"I'm going out now to look at the fish," Skipper Joe said. "It's getting pretty hot outside, so I may have to turn them over before they sunburn."

"You go on," Molly said. "I'll be all right."

The skipper left to take care of the fish. Molly could feel the pains coming again, as if something were about to burst inside her. The pain! She couldn't bear it any longer. She started crying loudly, and not wanting the skipper to hear her, she put a corner of the blanket in her mouth and bit down on it.

She felt something break inside her, and there was a release of muscle tension as she felt a burning liquid coming from between her legs.

"Oh, my!" she screamed. "I think I'm having a baby!"

Her mind raced to the time when she had heard her mother and aunt talking about the time when one of them had a baby. They had said things like "I knew it when my water broke. I only had three or four pains. It was only minutes." Now these words were becoming a reality for Molly.

"Yes," she said again, "I'm going to have a baby!"

Then she thought, *No, it takes nine months to grow a baby.* "Maybe I'm going to have one of those..."

She didn't know what to call it, but she knew that her water had broken.

Molly tried to get out of the cramped bunk but couldn't. She put her hands down and felt the liquid that had pooled between her legs. She couldn't tell if the wetness was water or blood, until she pulled her hand back from beneath the blankets. It was bloody.

"I'm finished," she whispered.

Molly resolved there and then to keep her shame a secret. *I'll never tell anyone. No one will ever know.*

The pain gripped again her as she started pushing, a natural reaction. It took only a few minutes for her to have the premature child, but the pain was still terrible. *I'm dying! My, oh my, I'm dying!*

Sometime later, Skipper Joe came inside and saw her crying. He couldn't see the mess that Molly had concealed with her blanket, but the lack of colour in her face frightened him.

Before he knew it, the old man blurted out his fears. "Oh, Molly, my dear, you have typhoid fever. I knew it, I knew it! You caught it from the captain yesterday. What can I do? I'm going to have to go somewhere and get medicine for you."

Molly knew it wasn't typhoid fever, but if the skipper and his crew thought it was, they might never suspect that she was pregnant and had had a baby. This thought gave her some emotional relief, but the pain began again. Nausea struck, and she passed out.

Everyone familiar with the history of Newfoundland is well aware of the terrible conditions that existed along the Labrador during the mid- and late 1800s. Up to 1892, when Dr. Grenfell arrived on the Labrador coast, and for a few years after that, many people had never seen a medical doctor in their entire lives. This made the job of any doctor arriving in the area ten times harder. Dr. Grenfell recorded that most of the elderly people he treated died, because by the time he treated them they were so sick and so far gone that it was impossible to restore their health. Also, most were so obsessed with home remedies that it was a job to educate them. With the younger men and women it was a little easier, especially when it came to child-bearing. However, opportunities to educate them were scarce, since hospitals and nursing stations and medicines were few and far between.

Is it any wonder, then, that when Skipper Joe Budden heard Molly crying and screaming in agony, it frightened him to the very depths of his soul? If Dr. Grenfell himself found it hard to keep medicines in stock, they would have been virtually non-existent in that little cabin at Indian Tickle.

Skipper Joe trudged down to the fish stage, in such despair he was nearly too weak to stand up. He was convinced that Molly had typhoid fever. If Molly had taken sick just twenty-four hours earlier and had the miscarriage, he wouldn't have been able to blame it on typhoid fever. She wouldn't have come in contact with the Nova Scotian fishing crew, and he wouldn't have overlooked the obvious. Fate was against them.

"What can I give her? What can I do?" he asked the empty sky. "Do I have anything in our medicine box aboard the schooner, I wonder?" He stepped aboard the small rowboat and rowed out to the schooner to check on his medical supplies.

There was Radway's Ready Relief, liniment and ointment, some old pills he didn't recognize, Epsom salts, and senna tea. That was all. Skipper Joe thought about readying the schooner and setting sail for home, but decided against it. If Molly had typhoid fever and was moved, it would mean sudden death for her, and the rest of the crew would catch it. It crossed his mind that Jack might have courted her the night before. If she caught it when the Nova Scotian captain kissed her and Jack kissed her afterwards, he was guaranteed to have the germ.

The thought nearly drove him crazy. "I'm finished. We're all finished! God help us!"

It was late in the afternoon when Skipper Joe's fishing crew entered the little harbour. There were four men at the oars, and a fifth at the sculling oar. He knew they had a fair catch for the day, because the boat was low in the water. Usually, when they arrived from fishing all day, they would immediately head to the cabin for a hearty meal prepared by Molly. After a feed, they would go to the schooner to clean, split, and salt their catch. By that time it would be almost dark, and they would return to the cabin and retire for the night. This routine was about to come to an end.

As the crew came farther into the harbour, they saw the skipper on board the schooner. He was waving for them to come to him, so they complied. As they came alongside, Skipper Joe was solemn.

Bill asked, "What's the matter?"

The skipper remained silent as Bill tied the boat on.

The others spotted their bedding on the deck of the schooner. They looked at the old skipper in wonder, and Bill spoke for them all. "Why are our mattresses on the deck? What's going on?" Just a few moments earlier, they had been talking about how hungry they were and ruminating over the great meal that Molly was sure to serve them, but the look on the skipper's face said something was very wrong.

Roy cleared his throat. "What's happened, Father?"

The old man choked on his words. "Molly has typhoid fever."

Everyone stared at him, shocked and bewildered.

"How do you know that, Father?" Roy demanded. "How do you know that she has typhoid fever?"

Finally, the old man found the words. "She's up there in the cabin, burning up with a fever and turning dark, and I think she's dying. She has all the symptoms of typhoid, and I should know because I had it once myself."

The six men stood dumbfounded as they stared toward the tarpaper-covered shack that had been their summer home. Each man now realized why the skipper had signalled them to board the schooner: they couldn't go back to the cabin for fear of catching the disease.

Jack spoke up. "Father, how sure are you?"

"I'm one hundred per cent sure. Listen, Jack, when Captain Edwards went to the cabin, he gave Molly a five-dollar bill and gave her a hug and a kiss. Something told me at the time that it was bad news."

Jack was silent. He thought about Molly and how much he loved her. She had told him in a frightened voice, *I'm going to have a baby, Jack.*

The words echoed in his head. Just last night he had told her that they would get married as soon as they got back home to Seldom-Come-By.

His brother Bill spoke up, breaking Jack's train of thought. "To hear that captain coughing and barking yesterday evening was enough to convince me that he was a very sick man."

Everyone murmured consent.

Roy nodded. "We were talking about it today when we were out fishing. That is one schooner that will soon be drifting with no one alive on board. That was a sick-looking crew on her."

"What do we do now, Father?" Bill asked.

"You won't be able to go back to the cabin. You're going to have to stay here aboard the schooner. That's why I brought out your gear. I'll be cooking for you and looking after Molly. I'm warning all of you that you are not to go into the cabin for anything, because if anyone catches it and brings it back to the schooner, it'll be death for all of you."

They all believed it, remembering all too well yesterday evening, when they had buried two men stricken with the fever. As if on cue, they looked toward the hillside and the crosses that stabbed the late afternoon sky like crooked fingers.

Skipper Joe cleared his throat. "I have your supper cooked for you down in the forecastle. Hurry up and eat, and get back on deck so this fish doesn't spoil."

There was nothing the crew could do for Molly. To a man, they were in a melancholy state, since each loved her in his own way.

At the time Molly became sick, Dr. Grenfell was in the northernmost part of Labrador, "way down north" in the little Inuit village of Hebron. In this native town was a large Moravian Mission establishment which was very supportive of Grenfell. Even if Skipper Joe had known the doctor was there at the time, Hebron was too far north to be contacted to come to Molly's aid.

The skipper settled the crew away for the night, and with the day's catch secured in the hold, each man washed and went below while the skipper went ashore to look after Molly. He walked to the cabin very quietly, listening for sounds inside, but all was still. He carried a small dish of cooked beans that he had brought in from the schooner, figuring that solid food would make her feel better.

The first thing he heard upon entering was a pained groan. Skipper Joe placed the dish on the table and went into the bedroom where Molly lay. She looked very pale, with sweat on her forehead and her hair matted onto her face.

"How are you, Molly, my dear?"

At first he thought she didn't hear him, and before he could ask again, she opened her eyes. They were dull and glassy. She mumbled, "Not good, sir."

"Do you still have a headache?"

"Yes, sir," she replied.

Molly had been suffering terribly all evening. Her stomach throbbed, and the pain was excruciating. She didn't have the dreaded typhoid fever, but she would never be able to relate this to the skipper. It was a problem with her pregnancy; the discharge of blood from her body confirmed her worst fears. She could feel the blood and water soak the mattress right up to her shoulders as she lay in the bunk. She was so distraught that she didn't care if she lived or died.

When there was no one around, Molly had uncovered herself and taken a look at the whole mess; she was horrified at what she saw. There was blood everywhere, all the way down to her knees. She knew she was in deep trouble.

She had cried in despair, "I want to die! Dear God, I want to die! I'm afraid I'll be found out! I want to die!"

To ask for a doctor or nurse or even a midwife didn't enter her mind. After she had covered herself with the heavy blankets and closed her eyes, she again asked the Great Maker to take her away.

Skipper Joe had no idea Molly had suffered a miscarriage. If she had told him what her exact trouble was, he would have personally taken her, body and bones, and loaded her on the schooner and headed out to the nearest community to find a midwife or anyone else to help her. He would even have tried to tackle her medical problem himself, had he known.

This kind-hearted man (Grenfell's phrase for Captain Budden) wouldn't have worried about what anyone said. In fact, no one back home would have discovered what her trouble was, because he would charge his men not to say anything about it, and they wouldn't have. Alas, Molly kept it from him, in fear of how she would be judged. She kept her hands down inside the covers in case there was any telltale blood on them, because if the skipper saw it he would demand answers from her.

Molly felt as though she were burning up. She knew she had a fever, and her head felt as if it would explode. "I think I'm going to faint, sir," she said in a low voice.

"Wait a minute. I'll get a cold wet cloth," Skipper Joe said as he hurried out of the bedroom. In a moment he was back with a wet washrag. He placed it on her forehead.

"Thank you, sir, that feels better." Then she remembered something. "Oh my, I haven't prepared the men's supper yet, Skipper," she said, alarmed.

"Molly, don't you worry about the men's supper. I had it ready for them when they came in."

"Where are they, Skipper? Are they in from fishing yet?"

"Yes," he answered. "They had a lot of fish, and it's all put away."

"Where are they?" she pressed.

"They're staying out on the schooner tonight. They didn't want to disturb you, seeing you have the typhoid fever."

Molly was shocked at the thought of the men being cooped up on the little schooner just because they thought she had typhoid fever. She cried harder.

What am I going to do? she thought. *Should I tell the skipper the truth and suffer the consequences when I get back home?*

No, she couldn't, no matter what happened. Seldom-Come-By would be alive with talk and rumours, and everyone would look down on her father and mother if it were found out. Molly went over it in her mind a thousand times as she lay there. People would say, "What kind of creature is she? As soon as she was out of her mother's sight, she crawled in with the men." Others would say what a tramp she was. "Couldn't even go down cooking on the Labrador without getting in the family way." She would be condemned forever.

"I want to die!" she screamed.

The old man looked on, helpless to cure her body or her mind. He held the wet cloth on her forehead and pleaded. "Oh, Molly, my dear, don't say things like that! You'll be all right. The fever should leave you in twenty-four hours. You're strong and young, and you can overcome this, I'm sure you can. I had the typhoid fever once, just like you. I survived it, and surely you will, too."

Molly's tears spoke of the doubt in her heart.

TEN

Dr. Grenfell sat in the *Albert's* cabin with Captain Trezise. They had a long talk about what was needed and what they would like to see along the Labrador coast. "It's not only medical help these people need," Grenfell said. "It's education, and that includes all the people from the Quebec border to the very tip of northern Labrador. But what puzzles me the most is that the people coming from the island part of Newfoundland appear to be the most illiterate and worse off."

"I agree," said the captain.

The doctor went on to talk about the fish merchants and what they were doing with the people, especially along the tip of the Great Northern Peninsula and the Labrador coast.

"It's mind-boggling," Captain Trezise agreed.

Grenfell thought for a moment. "Looking at the whole picture, I think the greatest need is for nursing stations or hospitals in the most vital, centralized areas, supported by a hospital ship."

Trezise nodded. "Where will the money come from to build the nursing stations and hospitals and to hire staff?"

"We would have to raise the money from somewhere and look for volunteers from back home and the United States, or maybe Canada," Grenfell explained. "It's September now; I think we should work our way back south along the coast and decide where the stations should go. In other words, we'll look at the most populated areas where the fishermen live aboard their schooners or have summer stations.

"There's one thing we know for sure, and that is, north of the Lake Melville inlet, the Moravian Mission has at least something to offer the people up there. They only need doctors, nurses, and a better supply of medicine. Their facilities are very good, but it's south of the Lake Melville inlet where the greatest problem lies. That's the most populated area, and there's absolutely nothing there. We should set sail immediately and do a survey of the complete coast south of here. What do you think?"

"I think you're right, Wilfred," the captain said. "We can leave right away."

"We should go south as far as Red Bay, and from there work our way back north. This will give us a chance to talk to as many people as possible before they leave for home on the island. From Red Bay we can head out straight for Battle Harbour and make that our first stop."

"Yes," Trezise said. "Here's what I'll do: I'll head straight off from the coast, clear of everything, and go straight southwest. That way we'll have little interference. It's the fastest way; if all goes well, we should make the trip in less than twenty-four hours."

"Great," said the young doctor, and the captain turned and went on deck.

The *Albert* sailed into the little town of Battle Harbour with all her sails glowing in the afternoon sun. They had made it in less than a day, as predicted by the captain.

The hospital ship dropped anchor in the harbour. After her sails were lowered, the crew caught sight of a beautiful sloop tied to the wharf. A sign on a building nearby read BAINE JOHNSTON AND CO LTD.

"It's good to see a little advertising again, Captain."

Trezise smiled. "The sloop in there is not a fishing craft, for sure, Doctor. It's too clean and tidy." The name written on the small ship was *Petrel*.

"Yes, it must be a visitor. I wonder who that could be?"

Grenfell was anxious to get ashore and find out more details about the little town and its people. He was also anxious to get his feet on dry land again.

"Let's get the boat in the water, men," the captain said.

It wasn't long before the little boat was heading for shore, with the doctor and captain aboard. As they neared the wharf, a group of curious people greeted them. They caught the lines and helped the visitors up. Dr. Grenfell took the lead in introducing everyone to them.

One of the men asked, "Are you the doctor that my brother met in the spring outside the harbour when they were fishing? You know, the one that gave him the baccy?"

Grenfell shook hands with him and said, "Yes, we certainly are, sir. We remember them quite well, because they gave us some of those delicious salmon. He was very kind; we'll never forget him."

The man was pleased to hear the doctor's kind words. He beamed with pride.

"We'll be holding a medical clinic in half an hour, so you can spread the word around."

Everyone was glad to hear it. One man immediately spoke up and said, "My mother is very sick, Doctor! I wonder if you could come to the house and see her now? She can't get out of bed. I can take you to her."

Grenfell replied, "Just as soon as I get my medical bag we'll go to her."

He immediately began the task of calling on each house. He was inside one of the livyers' homes when Captain Trezise came looking for him.

"Dr. Grenfell," he said, "when you're finished here, I'd like you to come back to the wharf. There's someone who'd like to talk to you. He says it's important."

"Okay, Captain, as soon as I'm done I'll be right over." The captain thanked him and left. Grenfell knew that it must be urgent for the captain to come looking for him. When he finished examining and treating his patient, he went outside.

A man on the wharf introduced himself as John Croucher. "I'm the company manager, Doctor."

"How are you? I'm Dr. Grenfell."

"I'm fine, thank you. Mr. Grieve—that's Mr. Walter Grieve, the company president—is here in Battle Harbour and would like to meet you. He would like you to come to the staff house for tea."

"I certainly will," said Grenfell. "What time does he prefer?"

Croucher said, "He'd like you to come now, if at all possible, because he's travelling on the fisheries patrol boat the *Petrel*. Their plans are to leave port as soon as possible, because her captain wants to get across the strait before dark. There's a storm brewing for tomorrow."

"Okay," the young doctor said, "I'll go and see him now."

Croucher was pleased. He led Grenfell to the staff house of Baine, Johnston and Company, to meet the president, Mr. W. B. Grieve. Grenfell took a look around. What a difference this place was from the squalid huts he had just left, where he had visited the sick! Old women had been lying on bags of feathers for mattresses, and sick youngsters sprawled on bare boards covered in old coats that looked like they had been worn on the battlefield in some ancient war. But here, everything was clean and painted; the house was well built, with factory-made furniture. Grenfell went into the main sitting room, in the centre of which was a large, round oak table of the latest design, surrounded by matching high-backed chairs.

Sitting at the table was Walter B. Grieve, unaware that Grenfell had arrived.

Croucher cleared his throat politely. "Excuse me, Mr. Grieve." Grenfell detected respect, perhaps fear, in Croucher's voice.

Grieve turned around, beholding for the first time the English doctor whom the governor had talked about. He was genuinely glad to see this young physician. "Well, Dr. Grenfell, how are you?" he asked, holding out his hand. "I'm Walter Grieve, and I'm at your service."

Grenfell gave him a hearty handshake, at once realizing that this man was a Scot. Grieve offered him a chair at the table. The doctor thanked him and sat down.

"You are from Scotland, if I'm not mistaken, Mr. Grieve. I think I recognize the accent."

"Yes, I'm from Glasgow," Grieve said with a grin. Here was a man of authority, Grenfell thought.

Grieve turned to Croucher. "Tell Miss Greene to come in, please."

"Yes, Mr. Grieve," he said politely, and disappeared into the kitchen.

Shortly, a young lady dressed in kitchen attire entered the room. When she saw the young doctor, she was taken by surprise. "Yes, Mr. Grieve, what can I do for you?"

"Miss Greene, I want you to meet Dr. Grenfell. He's the young doctor we've all heard of. Now he is here in person."

"I'm pleased to meet you, Miss Greene," Grenfell said, offering his hand. Years later, in telling the story of how she met the doctor, Jemima Greene said that the doctor swept her off her feet from the first time he spoke.

"Thank you, sir," she said, wide-eyed. "What can I get you, gentlemen?"

"I'll have a cup of tea, please," Grenfell said.

Grieve ordered coffee for himself, and Miss Greene went off to the kitchen.

"Doctor, when you were in St. John's this spring, or this summer, I should say, I was not fortunate enough to have met you. I suppose it was due to the big fire. However, since then I have talked to the governor on different occasions, and he told me about you and your mission. As I said to him, I say to you now: we are excited to have you here on the Labrador. We both agreed that the Old Country is still on the right track, you know."

Grenfell knew what England was allowing the fish merchants to do with its citizens in the colony, but he kept his thoughts to himself. Walter Grieve didn't know that he was talking to one of the future's greatest pioneers, who would one day fight for the poor and destitute and cause his business empire great concern. It made no sense for Grenfell to confront Grieve with his thoughts on human rights and the truck system. It was better to stay quiet and work with the man as much as possible and see what he had to offer.

"This area around here, Doctor," Grieve said, "around Battle Harbour, has the greatest potential on the Labrador, you know. This year we have increased our business by one hundred per cent, and we hope to expand again when we come back in the spring."

Grenfell accepted a cup of tea from Miss Greene. It was obvious that she was both cook and serving lady, and Grenfell estimated her age to be around twenty-five. Grieve stopped his conversation and focused his attention on the young cook when he saw his guest's interest in her. "Miss Greene is a wonderful cook, Doctor."

The young lady blushed and winked at Grenfell when Grieve wasn't looking. She had heard of Grenfell, but never thought that she would meet such a handsome man. He responded to her wink with the most beautiful smile she had ever seen.

Miss Greene left, and Walter Grieve looked his guest in the eye. "Doctor, I haven't got much time. The glass is showing bad weather coming up, so I'll get right to the point. I want to make a proposal to you. I know that you must be dedicated to the Labrador or you wouldn't be here. Therefore, I'm offering you this house as a nursing station or as a hospital, free of charge for five years as of today's date. All of its contents will stay in the house as you see it now, and Miss Greene will be at your disposal and paid a salary out of my own resources, five dollars per month for five years. She has been our cook and caretaker for a good many years."

Grieve sipped his coffee and continued. "Dr. Grenfell, I would like to have your answer before I leave, because if you accept we will have to make the necessary arrangements to prepare another building for our staff for next year."

Dr. Grenfell had difficulty comprehending what he had just heard. Walter Grieve took great delight in seeing Grenfell's surprise at this news. "I-I accept your generous offer, Mr. Grieve. However, I would like to arrange a meeting with you to discuss it further when I get back to St. John's later this fall."

"That will be fine," said Grieve.

"We'll work out the details and put them on paper. As you know, the Mission is an organization with no business arrangements of any kind, only charitable work by volunteers."

"I'm quite aware of that, Doctor. You can draw up your own contract. The cost for five years' rent will be one dollar, and I will pay that."

It was almost too much for Dr. Grenfell to believe!

"And to make things easier for you," said Grieve, "we will do the maintenance on the building during the five years."

"You are certainly very generous, Mr. Grieve."

"Call me Walter."

"Walter it is. God must have sent you from heaven. Never in my wildest dreams did I think this would happen, especially here in Labrador."

"I have one condition that I hope will be easy for you to accept," Grieve continued. "All I ask is that in the contract you draw up, you include a commitment on your part that you will operate a nursing station or hospital here with staff for a minimum of five years. At the end of five years, we'll talk again."

The businessman stood and walked to a cabinet near the fireplace. He took down a ring with keys on it and handed it over to Grenfell. "Jemima," he called, "would you come here, my dear?"

Miss Greene came immediately. "Yes, Mr. Grieve?" she asked.

"I want you to meet your new boss, Dr. Grenfell. He will be operating a hospital here in this house for the next five years, or perhaps longer, beginning right away."

Miss Greene's jaw dropped. "I'll be as faithful to you, Doctor, as I was to Mr. Grieve."

Grenfell laughed and thanked her as Grieve started gathering his effects. "She'll be the caretaker this winter, as usual. You don't have anything to worry about; she's better than any man."

"I'm without words to thank you enough, Walter. This will be a new beginning for the people of Labrador and the fishermen who come north every spring. I'm sure that the Mission for Deep Sea Fishermen will be more than pleased when they hear this news."

"Not at all! It is we who should be thanking you. It's the least I can do, since the need is great."

"It's a giant step forward, and something that will never be forgotten," said the young doctor.

Walter Grieve nodded and said, "When you come to St. John's on your way home, I want you to come directly to my home. We'll have dinner with the governor and the prime minister. At my expense, of course." They laughed.

Grieve took his bag and left Grenfell under Miss Greene's wing, in the first hospital in Labrador. She took Grenfell on a tour through the building, inspecting each room, including the kitchen and storage areas. The survey took about an hour, and when he went down to the wharf, the *Petrel* was gone.

The doctor met Captain Trezise on the wharf. "I want to see you in the cabin, Captain. I have good news for you."

In private, the doctor bubbled with excitement as he told the captain of Walter Grieve's offer of the staff house. "He even offered us a woman, his best employee, and is paying her to cook for us for five years."

"Santa Claus of Labrador, that's what he is," laughed Trezise.

"It's almost too good to believe," said the young doctor, shaking his head.

They renewed their plans of locating other stations along the coast. Grenfell said, "Tomorrow morning we should head north again and go as far as Cartwright, maybe do a few clinics on the way there and talk to the people who are left on the coast. By now most of the fishermen from the south have gone home for the winter."

"Okay," said the captain. "If the weather is all right in the morning, we'll head north again."

"Good. I think I'll spend a night at the staff house and let the people know what's going on. I'll hold a clinic after dinner. What do you think?"

"That would be wonderful," said Trezise.

Grenfell felt on top of the world. Thousands of prayers had been answered this day.

ELEVEN

Skipper Joe Budden sat, alone and distraught, in the corner of the shack stuck on the cliffside. All day and night he was up with Molly. Sometimes she was wide awake and could talk to him, but most of the time she was unconscious or delirious and talking old foolishness.

The skipper thought, *The typhoid fever got her, and it's only a matter of time before she'll die.*

He sat and listened to her calling out to Jack, day and night, but he wouldn't dare let his son know, for fear that he'd come to her and catch his death. What puzzled him most was that when she was deep in delirium she would talk about a baby and call Jack's name.

"Oh my, Jack, the baby, the little baby," she would say, and call for the skipper's son. Skipper Joe would pull the screen across and leave her to herself, and when she quieted down he would go back into her room and put wet cloths on her forehead.

It was so hot in the small bedroom that he decided to saw a small hole in the side of the shack and install another window, just over Molly's bed. This allowed more light and helped air the room of the terrible odour that had developed in the last few days. He had heard that typhoid fever was capable of manifesting many bad things, but the stench was too much for him, and it had forced him out. Molly had been bedridden for eleven days and hadn't eaten anything. Sometimes she would sip a little water, and once she drank a little lime juice, but nothing else. She hadn't gotten out of bed and wouldn't let the skipper even touch the blankets on her, let alone help her to get on the pail to urinate or have a bowel movement. With the smell in the room, Skipper Joe knew she must be in an awful mess.

The odour was so bad that he hated going into the room. Molly didn't want him to come into the room anyway, so he sat outside, looking in at her frail body, helpless and wondering how long she had left on earth. He did go in once to brush away the flies. There seemed to be thousands of them, buzzing around her and crawling out from under the bedclothes, but for reasons known only to her, Molly wouldn't let him come near enough to expose her and clean her.

Skipper Joe blamed it all on himself.

He hadn't been fishing now for close to two weeks. His crew had been doing pretty well, but if he'd gone out in the boat with them, for sure he would have caught his share and helped to make the voyage a paying trip. If they didn't get a full load, the bills wouldn't be paid and there would be no food to eat during the winter, only the dole from the government, and six cents a day per person meant starvation.

"I don't know what I'm going to do!" he cried in despair.

For comfort he would pray. "Dear God, don't let me go out of my mind. I'm only a frail man." This prayer was for himself, but before the Amen he would include a petition to God for Molly.

After his prayer, he would begin to feel calm again. *I have to carry on,* he thought.

Jack was having a rough time of it. He knew that Molly was pregnant. She had told him so, but with the supposed typhoid fever, his father wouldn't permit him to see her under any circumstance. His brothers also warned him. "It's certain death to go up there, Jack. What's going to happen will happen," they would say. The thought of the disease frightened him and everyone else.

I wonder if the baby she's carrying will survive? Jack wondered. He would just have to wait, and hope that tomorrow his father would have good news for them.

On the morning of the fourteenth day, Skipper Joe was on his feet early. He hadn't slept at all the night before. Molly had cried and moaned all night, and she hadn't been sensible for two days. She couldn't last much longer, and the skipper was in a very bad state of mind himself. His tired body was slowly deteriorating; he wasn't very hardy at the best of times, and he had lost weight and felt ill. Only yesterday, Bill had told him he looked like someone cheating death, and sometimes he felt like it. He lit the fire and put the kettle on the stove to boil for tea.

Day was dawning when he looked at the weather glass. "We're going to have a blow today. I think I'll tell the boys." He put his boots on and went outside, but he was too late. The crew was just going around the point, headed for the fishing grounds. "God help them and God help me. The sky looks fair and the ocean is calm now, but the weather glass is dropping, and that's bad news."

His back bent with fatigue and worry, Skipper Joe Budden staggered back into the cabin. The kettle was boiling, sending steam halfway across the cabin, and Molly's moaning made his heart ache. Today there would be no peace.

From Battle Harbour the *Albert* sailed into Cartwright, where Dr. Grenfell held a clinic on board. He discovered that Cartwright was a place where a great number of Labrador people lived or visited year-round, so he placed it high on the priority list of sites for a hospital. Cartwright could potentially become a key medical centre on the Labrador coast.

The weather glass on the *Albert* showed that a storm was brewing. During the night, the doctor and the captain talked to a lot of people and were informed that most of the people had now gone back to the island of Newfoundland. Therefore, between Cartwright and Domino all the people were gone, so it was decided to make a run directly to Domino.

As they were preparing to leave, a man came to the wharf looking for the doctor. During the night his wife had gotten terribly sick. Dr. Grenfell went to his home and examined her, determining that she was suffering from food poisoning. This delayed the *Albert* from leaving Cartwright until about 10:00 A.M., at which time the captain came on deck and updated him. "The wind is starting to come on from the northeast, Doctor, but it shouldn't be too bad. If it gets too rough we can always steam in around the islands near Indian Tickle somewhere, or go up into one of the bays and anchor."

They encountered fair winds as they went around the west cape at the headlands. The *Albert* sped across the water as the northeast wind picked up in intensity and developed into a raging storm.

"I hope there's no one caught out in this, or it could be goodbye," said the captain.

Dr. Grenfell said, "Not many people go out this time of year, only those fishing alongshore. One of the men told me that, so I'd say that there's no one out."

Captain Trezise nodded and took a quick look around. He said, "I think we'll get in out of this. It looks like snow to me."

It had been a terrible morning for Skipper Joe. Molly was crying out to Jack and her mother. The old man was nearly out of his mind. "Only for the grace of God, I think I would have gone crazy," he would say later. This morning he was stumbling around the cabin, barely able to stand on his feet. Molly couldn't last much longer, and the thought broke his heart.

At around 9:00 A.M. the skipper checked on her and found that her breathing was irregular, her breath coming and going in rattles. It appeared that her lungs were filling up. "I think she's coming down with pneumonia," he mumbled. Fifteen days had passed since she had taken sick, and she hadn't eaten or drunk anything, or made an effort to get out of bed to make her water. It was unbelievable, but what was most puzzling was the fact that the typhoid fever hadn't taken her life yet. Skipper Joe was beginning to have doubts.

"If she doesn't have it, what could be wrong?" he asked himself.

During the night, he'd made up his mind that when the boys came back from fishing he was going to have Bill and Fred take her out of bed to clean her up. It would be a dirty task, but it was the least that could be done. He also decided that they would start preparing to go home. They might be able to complete their fishing efforts back home in the Seldom area. Using trawls and baited handlines, they just might strike a bit of luck.

Skipper Joe's thoughts were interrupted by Molly's moans. As he entered her room, a terrible stench filled his nostrils, and he figured that her flesh must be rotting. He'd smelled something like it before around home when a dead animal was found in the sun, festering for weeks.

"Molly, my dear, can you hear me?"

"Yes, Captain, I can hear you," she said, very low.

"You must try and drink something, my dear. Do you want a cup of tea?"

She whispered, "No, sir."

Skipper Joe put his trembling hand on her forehead, and, thinking he'd heard her say something, put his ear close to her mouth. "What is it, Molly?" he asked.

Very faintly, he heard her say, "Mother...I want Mother."

The words cut the old man to the heart. Molly was crying out for her family. What could he say or do?

Swallowing the lump in his throat, he said, "Molly, tomorrow morning we're going home. Just as soon as we can get our stuff aboard the schooner, we'll be leaving."

The skipper's promise was lost on her. She hadn't heard him. If she had, she would have protested and repeated her wish to die.

Another worry began to impose its presence, and for some time it pushed the skipper's concern for the girl to one side. Was the wind—yes, the wind was blowing. He went to the window and looked out. "The wind has pitched," he said.

Skipper Joe rubbed his eyes and looked again at the weather glass. "The storm is on. I wonder where the boys are?"

It had been a calm morning, with a little sea rolling, so it didn't take the crew long to row the six miles to the fishing grounds. They had fair catches with the trawls, striking fish every time the baited hooks got near the bottom.

Jack and Gid worked alone in the trap skiff, side by side, and had moved apart from the others in the dories. "I have a feeling that it's going to blow today," Gid remarked.

"There's a lot of fish here," said Jack, ignoring Gid's concerns about the weather.

"Listen to me, will you, Jack?" Gid said, irritated. "We're going to have a storm of wind. I can tell by the way the clouds are forming up there." He pointed to a group of clouds that were scudding very fast in over the land.

Jack peered at the ominous clouds. "Did anyone look at the weather glass this morning?"

"No, your father won't let anyone go close to the cabin anymore, even to look at the weather glass."

"Poor Molly. I wonder how she is this morning?"

Gid stopped what he was doing. He sighed, then turned to Jack. "Listen, we might as well face the facts this morning."

Puzzled, Jack looked at Gid and wondered why he would make such a statement. "What do you mean, Gid?"

"You know full well, Jack, that Molly doesn't have typhoid fever."

Jack's mind raced. He hadn't said a word to anyone about what Molly had told him of her being in the family way, and he didn't know if Gid was trying to get information out of him. "I don't know what you're talking about, Gid."

109

"Oh, yes you do, Jack. You know all about Molly being in the family way."

"What...are you saying, Gid?"

Gid didn't know the right words to describe the situation. "I'm saying that Molly has had a baby, or part of a baby. One of them...I don't know what it's called. You know. Anyway, it's one of them when a baby is born too soon, before its time."

Gid stared at Jack blankly. Jack stared back in silence. Finally, he said, "How do you know about Molly, Gid?"

"I have a confession to make. I'm going to your father to tell him that I'm the one who put her in the family way. Ever since she became bedridden, I've been feeling terrible about it. I'm sorry."

Jack took a step back. Gid and Molly! Should he believe him? Was it possible? Had Molly been with Gid behind his back? *No, no.* He didn't believe him—Gid was making it up. On the other hand, how did Gid know about it?

He was stuck for words. He knew that Molly was in the family way because she had told him, and he noticed her stomach getting bigger as the weeks went by. No, Jack was sure that Gid didn't know anything about Molly. It was just a lucky guess.

"You're a liar, Gid," he growled. "You haven't been with Molly."

Sensing his partner's anger, Gid knew a lot of trouble was about to start between himself and Jack if he didn't change the subject. He cleared his throat and said, "Listen, Jack, I was only kidding you. But Bill and Roy know about her. They've talked about how big she's been getting all the time. I heard them talking about it, and they blame it on you. You're going to have to go to your father when you get in and tell him."

Jack shook his head. "I know, but how can I do that, Gid? The old man will break my neck!"

"It has to be done, Jack. For Molly's sake."

"You're right. But the old man has enough trouble now, and if I told him about that, he would die for sure."

"It has to be done," Gid repeated.

110

"Maybe I could tell Bill about it and get him to tell the old man. He would handle it better."

Gid made no further comment, and the two men went back to work.

It took an hour before the wind really picked up from the northeast. It was now around 11:00 A.M. "I told you it was going to blow, Jack," said Gid. "My son, we're in for a bad storm."

"You could be right," Jack answered in an offhand manner as he hauled another large cod in over the gunwale of the boat. "Look, a big blower," he said, struggling to get the huge codfish aboard.

"Never mind the big blowers. The rain is coming, or worse. Maybe a snowstorm."

Jack said, "All right, I think we should signal the boys to let go of the trawls and come to the boat."

Gid put on his coat and stood upon the gangboards. He started waving to the crew.

"I think they see you, Gid."

"Yes, they see me, but it's going to take them close to half an hour before they get here. Why don't they put out their sail?"

"Don't worry, Bill will have it out."

"We may as well continue fishing until they get here."

"I guess so," said Jack.

"I'm worried because we still have six miles to row before we get to the land," Gid said as he started to pull up another large fish.

The wind was blowing strong by the time the two dories reached the trap boat, and a snow squall hovered over the land. The four men quickly transferred fish from the two dories into the larger boat, and soon enough the grapnel was hauled up and four oars were pulling hard to bring them to land.

"Hoist up the sail, boys," Bill ordered, shouting over the heavy rain and snow.

"Looks like the wind is going around to the southeast," said Roy. "Hand me that compass, someone, so I can get a shot at the land before visibility closes in."

"Listen, Roy, the land is already closed in. That happened before you got to the boat," Bill said.

"I know the direction, anyway. It's northwest."

"You're right," Bill said. He raised his voice. "Listen, boys, I'd say that before this day is over we could be in for a rough time. This is going to be a bad storm; it came on too fast to please me."

The six men got the sail up and took in their oars, because the wind was fierce. They were all nervous, because if they missed their small cove with this strong wind in on the land, it would be a job to get a sheltered place to ride out the storm, especially with no visibility. They had to get in behind one of the small islands, where they would be able to weather the worst storms Labrador could throw at them.

Bill was the most experienced when it came to the Labrador weather, and he knew that the storms from the southeast often switched to a deadly gale from the northwest. His main concern now was getting close enough to spot land before the wind changed.

The force of the southeast wind struck the *Albert* when she was about a mile off the outer point of the Cartwright headlands. "We'll have to take some of the canvas off her, boys," said Captain Trezise. He stood next to the rail, holding onto the spar cables for balance. His oilskins were battened down tight, protecting him from the driving rain and snow.

He would have to get his vessel into a sheltered cove somewhere, Indian Tickle if possible. But where was Indian Tickle? He couldn't see the land for blinding snow, but he knew the general direction since he had taken a compass bearing before losing sight of the shore. He would have to take a chance and make a run for it.

TWELVE

It appeared that Molly was unconscious, and Skipper Joe expected her to die at any time. Since the storm struck the cove, he had been walking the floor, blaming himself for not telling the boys that the weather glass forecast dirty weather. The wind had blown from the northeast before changing to the southeast, and it started to pick up into a mighty gale. If the crew paid attention to the weather signs, they still had enough time to get ashore, but he had no way of knowing how alert they were.

He kept his eyes focused in the direction of the small harbour entrance, because at that moment the rain and snow were so heavy that he couldn't even see that far. The sea was beginning to heave, and he knew that if the crew didn't get back soon they would have a perilous time getting in. The huge waves broke right across the harbour mouth, but Bill and Roy knew all about it, so it wasn't a big worry. Getting to the harbour mouth in this blinding snow and avoiding the outside cliffs was the big problem, and he had a feeling in his gut that there was going to be trouble. He looked toward the harbour entrance again and buried his face in his hands. "Where are they, I wonder? Oh, my, what will this day bring forth?"

Sometime around three o'clock, the skipper went into the small bedroom and sat down on the bench near Molly. The stench was overpowering, but he was so worried about other things that he paid no heed.

"Molly, my dear, can you hear me?"

He put his hand on her shoulder and gently shook her.

"Molly, can you hear me?" he repeated.

She opened her eyes a fraction. "Yes, sir," she murmured.

The old man was surprised to see she was still conscious. "Is there anything I can get for you?"

Molly rolled her head from side to side.

"Can I get you a drink of lime juice, my dear?"

"No, sir," she replied faintly.

Skipper Joe was sitting with his patient when he thought he heard something unusual, like the sound of chains rattling. He eyed the rain on the window, and then he heard it again, louder this time. Startled, he jumped to his feet. "What in the world is that?"

He ran to the window in the kitchen and looked out, squinting to adjust his eyes. "Something's there. I see our schooner, but what's that?"

The old man ran for the door, opened it and stepped out, not noticing the driving rain. "By Job, another schooner!"

For a moment he thought he was seeing things, and he went back into the cabin. At the window he could see better.

"Yes, 'tis a schooner, all right, and she's anchored." His eyes were glued to the deck, where men were running about, hauling ropes and working the chain hawser. "That was the chain I heard as she dropped anchor."

Skipper Joe left the window and donned his oilclothes. Then he ran for the stage. The wind was blowing a hurricane, and the rain came in sheets as he went inside and walked out on the stagehead to greet the men aboard the strange schooner. They waved to him and he waved back, his thoughts racing.

Who are they? I wonder if they have seen the boys? There's only one way to find out, and that is to go on board. He jumped from the wharf down into the small rowboat and put out the oars. The crew of the strange ship watched with curiosity from the deck.

As he rowed toward the ship, a question formed in his mind. *I wonder if this is the schooner with the doctor Captain Edwards was talking about—Dr. Grenfell?*

"I wonder," Skipper Joe whispered, rowing harder and with renewed hope. "Whoever they are, they may have seen the boys." The old man had so much on his mind that he hardly knew what he was doing. He stopped close to the small vessel and looked up to the rail at the men. They stared back with blank faces.

"Good day, fellas," he shouted above the roar of the wind.

"Good day, sir," someone replied. "I must say, it's not a very good day to be out, is it, Skipper?"

"No," said Skipper Joe. "Which way are you going? North or south?"

"South."

"Are you from Newfoundland?"

"No," said the man. "We are from England."

Skipper Joe felt his heart leap in his chest. He gaped at the man and for a moment couldn't speak.

The men sensed something was wrong. "This is a hospital ship with a doctor on board. Dr. Grenfell."

This was too good to be true! Skipper Joe stammered, "C-c-can I see the doctor?"

A distinguished-looking man leaned over the rail and said, "I am Dr. Grenfell, sir."

The skipper froze. This was no time to be nervous, so he stood up in the small punt, as steady as if it were on dry land. "Doctor, I'm Joe Budden, and up in our shack I have a very sick young girl. Would you please come and see her?"

He pointed to the shack onshore.

"I certainly can," said Grenfell. "Just wait a minute until I get my medical bag."

"Thank you, Doctor," said Skipper Joe, almost crying with relief.

In less than two minutes, Dr. Grenfell was at the railing dressed in his oilskins and with his medical bag in hand. He leaped from the railing of the *Albert* to the bottom of the small punt—he was getting used to this sort of thing.

"Captain Trezise," Grenfell called back the schooner.

"Yes?" his captain said at the railing.

"Keep a watch on deck in case I need assistance, please."

"Don't worry about that, Doctor," Captain Trezise replied.

"Thank you."

Skipper Joe and the doctor came to the little wharf. When they went into the fishing stage, they shook hands.

"I'm Dr. Grenfell. Pleased to meet you."

The old man took off his old sou'wester and said, "I'm Joe Budden. They call me Skipper Joe."

Grenfell heard something in the tone of this man's voice that made him want to ask him questions about his own health, but instead he pressed him for information about the patient. "How long has the young girl been sick, Captain?"

"Fifteen days, Doctor. I think she's dying." Skipper Joe's voice cracked on the last word. "But, Doctor, I have another problem now, a bigger one."

Grenfell blinked. "And what would be greater than this, sir?"

The young doctor heard fear in the skipper's voice. "Early this morning, my four sons and two other men went out on the banks fishing, and they're not back. They should've been back by twelve o'clock at the latest."

"We didn't see any strays on the water when we came in here. Maybe they went into another cove close by."

"No, Doctor, that can't be the case. Someone would have walked here to let me know about it. I'm so worried I'm sick."

"Maybe they'll get in before dark, sir," Dr. Grenfell said, but he could see the doubt in Skipper Joe's face. In silence, the two men started toward the shack.

Bill and Roy managed to control the trap skiff as they headed blindly toward the shoreline. The sea had gotten very rough, and the wind was so strong that there was no visibility at all.

"I don't know where we are, boys," Bill reported. "All we can do now is try and get in somewhere in the lun of the land, maybe in behind one of the islands."

Roy looked worried. It was very difficult to hear anyone above the wind and rain. Shouting back, he said, "The only thing I can say is we'd better get in the harbour before dark."

Bill warned, "Keep your eyes open for land, boys, and have the oars ready in case we have to keep her off the rocks."

They were just drifting in the wind, but the boat was stable. The six men were decked out from head to toe in their rubber clothes, which helped break the wind that pushed them closer and closer to the land.

At 3:00 P.M., they saw it. Gid was the first to spot the dark outline. "Jack, look, there's land right alongside!"

Bill was quick with the order. "Grab the oars, boys. Quickly!" Four of the men put their oars out and got the boat under their control, turning it in time to avoid a collision with the boiling sea and solid granite. The two small dories in tow almost smashed on the cliffs, but the men were quick enough to begin pulling them closer to the trap skiff.

Bill was relieved to see the dories coming in. "Pull harder on those oars, men," he roared. "Keep her off!" The men reacted immediately and pulled the skiff out of the shore breakers, just in time to avoid being grounded and tossed into the water.

"That was a close call," said Roy.

"Where do you think we are, Bill?" called Jack, concerned. "Do you recognize the shore?"

Bill looked at the seas foaming at the cliffs just fifty feet away. "I don't know where we are," he yelled above the roar of the sea. "Keep rowing, boys."

The oarsmen rowed savagely, and they rounded the point. "Keep her to the right, Bill, keep her to the right. Use the sculling oar," said Roy, rowing frantically. "Don't let her get in the undertow."

In a few minutes the boats rounded the sheltered side of the point of land, and Bill called for a rest. "Have a blow, and then get ready to move fast, because we can't stay here. The sea will eventually break right over this point."

He looked around. "This looks like an island to me. I think I know where we are. We should be just north of the point entrance to the harbour."

Gid looked to Bill for reassurance. "What should we do now? Should we throw out the grapnel, or what?"

"No, no, not here. We have to get out of this." The sea was wild, and everything was foaming. "'Tis a job to see, but we have to get out of here. It looks like..." Bill's voice trailed off.

"Looks like what?" Roy asked.

"Looks like the east island."

Roy frowned. "I'm not sure if it is."

The two dories were tied close to the trap skiff, and they bumped together angrily. Bill ordered, "Slacken one of those dories back from the other one so they don't beat each other up."

Bill got a better look at where they were. "I think we're in among the big shoals. If the snow would only let up for a minute we could see where we are, and we could do something."

But the air was thick with snow, and Bill knew it was no use complaining about the situation. It would only make it more difficult for everyone. The main thing was to stay calm and not panic, and try and get in the shelter as much as possible to wait out the storm.

The six men weren't worried about their physical condition. They were more than able to handle the snow and rain and the coming darkness, toughened as they were by a lifetime of hard work. It was the heavy sea rolling over the small island that worried them. There was only so much the boats could stand before being swamped or swept against the cliffs.

Finally, Bill said, "Listen, boys, we can't stay here. We have to get out clear of the breaking sea, so start rowing as hard as you can," He rocked the sculling oar with every ounce of strength he could muster.

"Where do you think we're going now, Bill?" asked Jack.

"I don't know, but anywhere is better than being tossed around here in this foaming sea, so row with all your might."

Ten minutes passed before they saw cliffs towering over them. "Another island—Bird Island," Bill said with relief. "We'll go in behind it and put out the grapnel." At least now he knew where they were. They would still need a lot of luck to survive, but knowing where they were was a little reassuring.

He knew it would be very tricky getting in through the breaking shoals to reach the shelter of Clummick Island. "Be careful, boys! Watch her now. Look at that big one coming there."

The six men braced themselves as a huge wave rolled under them and slammed against the cliffs.

The wind blew the breaking sea into flumes as thick as snowdrifts, and for awhile they rowed blindly through the foam. Ten more minutes passed, and they were now behind the Clummick, with just enough shelter for them to put the grapnel down. However, this was no place for a Sunday picnic. The ocean was alive and swirling. There were still many dangers in the raging storm of wind and rain and snow, and there was no way they could row the large, cumbersome trap boat and dories out around the exposed headland before making the sheltered harbour. At least they had their bearings and knew they weren't far from their little sheltered harbour. They could only wait it out and hope that the wind didn't change to the northwest.

"How wide is this tickle, Bill?" Jack asked.

"Not very wide, my son. I'd say a couple of hundred feet or so, maybe four hundred. And just over the hill is where the cabin is."

Jack knew he was right. "I know Father must be gone out of his mind by now. If only one of us could get ashore and get word to him." Molly was uppermost in his mind, but being the youngest in the family, he was very close to his father and worried constantly about him.

Bill nodded. "You're right, Jack, but we can't even see the land, and in this sea we can't move. We'll just have to sit and wait it out. We may have to wait 'til light tomorrow morning."

The men listened intently as Bill continued. "Brace yourself for a long night. Later on, if the wind dies down, and if we all call out together, we might be able to make enough noise for Father to hear us. You know how good his hearing is."

Jack grew despondent and thought of Molly, whom he figured was fretting over him, the father of their child. "What a life we have," he said. "What a dirty, rotten life this is."

With these words he slid down into the sheltered side of the boat.

THIRTEEN

As Skipper Joe and Dr. Grenfell walked the short distance to the cabin, the old man pointed to the two crosses on the hillside. "It all started from those two crosses up there, Doctor. The two men that I buried there died of typhoid fever. That's why Molly is sick now—she caught it from their captain."

By now the snow was coming down faster and the ground was covered. The skipper was going to tell Grenfell more about the Nova Scotian schooner's crew, when they reached the cabin. As they entered, Dr. Grenfell was met by a foul odour. Something was rotting very badly.

"What is that smell, Captain?"

Skipper Joe could hardly speak. "Doctor, it's coming from Molly." From the stress in his voice, Grenfell guessed the girl's condition was very serious.

The old man went into the small bedroom and looked at Molly. Her eyes were closed and she was motionless. Except for her breathing, a stranger would think she was dead. He laid his hand on her shoulder and said, "Molly. Molly, my dear. Can you hear me?"

She stirred.

"Molly, can you hear me?"

She opened her eyes. "Yes, sir, I can hear you."

Skipper Joe put his mouth to Molly's ear and whispered, "Dr. Grenfell is here to see you."

She didn't answer this time. Instead, she closed her eyes and turned her face toward the wall. Her long black hair was matted and hung limp over her face.

The skipper went out and spoke to the doctor. "You can go in and see her. I think she'll be able to hear you."

"Okay," said Grenfell, and he went into the small bedroom. It was beginning to get dark, and the doctor had difficulty examining his patient in the fading light. He returned to the kitchen again and said, "Captain, do you think that you can go out to our ship and get my lantern for me? I need a good light to work properly. It's very dull in that room."

"Yes, certainly, Doctor."

"I'll write a note for the captain because I'll be needing a few things, like rubber sheets and some disinfectant and other things. And tell Captain Trezise that I may not get aboard tonight."

"I'll be sure to tell him, Doctor," the old man said as he put on his raincoat.

Grenfell could see that this old gentleman was loaded down with worry, yet eager to jump and do anything that was asked of him. The young doctor gave him the note, and after stuffing it securely in his pocket, Skipper Joe stepped out into the rain and snow. With the hurricane of wind striking him in the face, he shut the door behind him and headed for the *Albert*.

The Budden crew were cold and wet as they tossed to and fro, sitting aboard the trap skiff anchored in the lun of the Clummick. It was getting dark, and they knew they were just holding on by their fingertips, each man expecting at any moment to be swept to his death in the pounding sea. Sitting exposed and without any kind of light, they had to be alert to spot any sign of greater danger. The two dories were at the ready, strung out behind the trap skiff, attached to each corner of the counter of the larger boat in case it was swept into the cliffs. Bill instructed them to throw away the day's catch of fish if the wind and sea changed direction. It would be a painful choice after their hard day of hauling it aboard, but, God willing, they wouldn't have to make it.

When the sun went down, the six men took turns eating lunch. They carried a galley, a homemade stove that burned wood to boil water and fry up food. After eating, they felt a little better, but the worry of having to spend the night in such a dangerous place was almost more than they could bear. Each man had the feeling that he was teetering on the edge of eternity.

Jack was thinking about Molly. He thought about what he was going to say to Bill about her being in the family way, and what he would want him to tell their father. And he was scared, wondering what would happen when his father found out that he had been hiding the truth and that the skipper had been wrongly treating Molly for typhoid fever. Skipper Joe and the dangerous sea weren't the only things that frightened him. Jack thought of Molly's relatives and friends back home, and how they would react if she died in the family way, and Jack being the cause of it. They'd consider him the murderer who made her pregnant and kept it hidden from everyone.

He would keep it a secret no longer. Jack resolved that when he got back into the harbour he was going to tell his father the truth about himself and Molly—that is, if they survived this ordeal, and their chances were slim. With a troubled mind, Jack Budden huddled in the side of the boat and buried his head in his arms to weep, silently, for Molly.

While Skipper Joe went to the *Albert* to get the supplies for Dr. Grenfell, the doctor went back in the room and sat down near his patient. He took her pulse and blood pressure. "You're a very sick young lady, Molly," he said. "Molly, do you hear me?"

She opened her blue eyes and looked at him.

Everyone who received medical and spiritual help from Grenfell had only good things to say about the doctor. Not only his personality attracted people to him, but his general manner and appearance, also. This feeling was shared by his patients and those who worked with him.

"You don't have typhoid fever, Molly."

Dr. Grenfell knew that the sailors on the Nova Scotian vessel didn't have typhoid fever; he had treated some of them for food poisoning while they were at Okak and Hebron, and this, no doubt, had caused their deaths.

Molly opened her eyes wider, and this time she focused on his face. He introduced himself again and was relieved to see that she wasn't frightened.

"Molly, I have to examine your stomach, so I'm going to remove the covers." She held onto the blankets defiantly, but eventually she let go and turned her head to the wall. Grenfell reached into his medical bag and took out a surgical mask and gloves. He put them on and slowly rolled back the soggy covers. Molly had rolled up the bottom of her long flannelette nightdress and used it as a sponge to soak up some of the blood and water and remnants of the partly developed child. Unable to disentangle her long nightdress, the doctor took his scissors and cut it off below her chest and down the sides, exposing her swollen, red stomach and releasing hundreds of flies. He felt her stomach and Molly winced in pain. He noticed her reaction and pushed a little harder. "Does this hurt, Molly?"

It was agony. "Yes."

The stench was so strong that Dr. Grenfell, years later, wrote "it appalled me." He cut away the rest of the nightdress and couldn't believe what he was seeing: the lower part of the young girl's body was infested with maggots.

Dear God, he said inwardly. *What a mess.* At once he understood the problem. He took Molly's hand in his and said, "Molly, some days ago you had a miscarriage and you have lost a lot of blood. But I am going to treat you and make you better."

Molly spoke slowly. "Don't let the skipper know, because he'll have to tell Mother and Father about it. Please don't let him know. He thinks I have typhoid." Fresh tears stood in her eyes.

"No, Molly, my dear, I'll not tell the captain. How long were you pregnant?"

"Three months," she replied weakly.

"Okay, Molly, you'll be fine. I'm going to clean and wash you, so just relax. In a minute I'm going to give you a little chloroform and this will make you sleep." Molly didn't know what chloroform was, but she trusted him completely.

Dr. Grenfell had great faith and wrote in his notes that "while there is life in a young patient, there is hope." He administered the chloroform and Molly immediately fell unconscious and felt no more pain. He suspected that she had been in severe pain ever since she'd had the miscarriage. When he thought of what she had gone through, he shuddered.

The doctor heard Skipper Joe coming up the walk, so he went back into the kitchen to greet him. The rain and snow pelted the outside of the cabin. "We're lucky to have a roof over our heads."

"Yes, Doctor."

"Is there any sign of your crew yet?"

"No, not a sign," the old man replied. "I asked your captain to blow his horn after dark. Maybe my crew will hear it."

"Yes, that's a great idea," said Grenfell. He could see that the skipper was distraught, but the job at hand was of greater concern. "Captain, I want you to move that table over near the door, and then we're going to get the patient out of bed. I'll also need lots of hot water."

"I have a large boiler pot of hot water on the stove now, Doctor."

"Good," Grenfell said. It was dark outside now. "You can light your lamp now, Captain, and mine also."

"Okay."

"I have sedated the patient, so she isn't feeling any pain. Please excuse me while I attend to her."

Skipper Joe didn't want to be left alone with his thoughts. He was convinced that Molly didn't have much of a chance at getting better—she had suffered too much for too long.

The doctor took the lantern and went back into Molly's room, placing it on the small bench before beginning his grisly task. He pulled back the sheet he had placed over her.

He rolled Molly's now-sedated form over to the wall, placed a rubber sheet on the bed, and rolled her back onto it. Next, he put a white sheet over her to protect her modesty from the skipper or anyone else who might look in.

Every few minutes a horn blew from the *Albert*. Skipper Joe would go to the door and open it to listen for any sound from his men, but none came. Grenfell came out of the room and saw that everything was neatly in place. Skipper Joe had moved the table close to the bedroom door and put a clean blanket over it.

"This is very good, thank you," the doctor said as he took another rubber sheet and spread it over the blanket on the table. "Now I want you to help me take Molly out of the bed and place her on the table. I don't think it'll be a very hard task, because she's very thin and frail."

The skipper was shocked at how far Molly had fallen. It seemed that only yesterday she was strong and healthy and active, full of life and energy. It took only a few seconds for the two men to lift the seriously ill girl from her bed to the table. The old man couldn't believe his eyes as he saw his young cook, his daughter, as it were, wrapped in a white sheet, to be butchered like a large codfish on the splitting table.

Dr. Grenfell suspected that Skipper Joe wouldn't have the heart to watch him wash and clean Molly. In fact, his plan was to keep the skipper away from the cabin, for fear of asking questions.

"You can go down to the stage if you like, Captain, and see if there are any signs of your crew."

Skipper Joe sensed the doctor didn't want him around.

"Yes, Doctor, that's a good idea," he said, and left.

126

As he went outside, he heard the horn of the *Albert* blow its mournful sound, struggling against the wind as it called out to the missing men behind the curtain of snow. Wherever they were, they must be frightened and cold, and the thought chilled Skipper Joe as he stumbled toward the wharf in the darkness.

The large trap skiff was still anchored in the shelter of Clummick Island. It bobbed up and down on the waves and swung back and forth on its anchor rope, holding on in the rough sea. Half an hour after nightfall, the six men were all watching and listening for anything that would give them a little shred of hope, when, in the depths of despair, Jack thought he heard a sound over the howling wind—a vessel's horn.

"Listen, I hear something," he said.

They looked at each other in astonishment, cocking their ears to verify Jack's claim. The muffling action of the snow and the roar of the sea made it difficult to hear, but after a minute of adjustment they heard it and recognized the sound. It was indeed a vessel's horn.

"Yes, I hear it!" Bill shouted.

He held up his hand as the horn blew again. "That way, there," he said, pointing in the direction of the sound. "It's coming from the harbour, but it doesn't sound like the horn on our schooner."

Roy nodded. "But it's in the harbour, that's for sure. It has to be the old man."

All hands were excited.

"If we only had a light," said Bill.

Gid shrugged. "We can't move anyway unless the weather lightens up. We can't see across the tickle."

Bill reassured Gid and the others. "It'll clear, and when it does, we'll make our move."

FOURTEEN

Dr. Grenfell removed the rubber and linen sheets from around Molly. He stripped off the top of her nightgown by cutting it with the scissors. He took the large fleshy mass from between her legs, unwrapping it from the lower folds of her nightgown. The fetus was still attached to her. There were maggots everywhere—it was unbelievable. He had seen some pretty awful sights as an intern, but this made him sick to his stomach. He removed the fetus and the afterbirth, cleaned up the maggots and crusted, dried blood, and washed her with disinfectant before firmly applying and fastening a large bandage between her legs. Grenfell knew from the redness and swelling that she had extensive internal infection.

Your hopes are very slim, he thought. Molly was still under the influence of the chloroform, so there was no danger of her hearing his greatest fears, but he didn't dare speak them aloud. He wrapped her in a warm blanket. Her pulse and heartbeat were very low, and she had very low blood pressure; Grenfell felt he was preparing her for her death, and he had to work hard to banish the thought from his mind.

Why is it I always get to these cases in time to watch them die? But I must think positively.

He stopped for a moment to pray. He would honour Molly's request—whether it was her last request or not, only time would tell—and let no one know about her pregnancy, which meant destroying the evidence. He would have to get the skipper to help take everything outside and burn it.

Grenfell was sitting at Molly's side when the skipper came back inside. The horn on the *Albert* was still blowing every so often. "There hasn't been any response from anyone out there, Doctor. I suppose they're driven off. If they were ashore anywhere, someone would have reached here overland by now."

Skipper Joe was worried sick about Molly. He kept glancing toward her curiously. She was so still she looked dead. "Is she alive, Doctor?"

"Yes, but barely. I would say that she is dying. I washed her and wrapped her in a warm blanket, and she is sedated. She is a very sick girl, Captain. I've put her to sleep with chloroform, and she may wake up in an hour. That is, if she wakes at all."

Dr. Grenfell cleaned up, and with the skipper's help he brought Molly back to her room.

The old man knew there was nothing he could do. Molly was in the hands of the doctor now, and in the hands of God. He tried to keep himself busy in order to take his mind off the missing men.

"Can I get you a cup of tea, Doctor?"

"Yes, I'd enjoy one very much," Grenfell replied.

The skipper lit a second lamp, allowing plenty of light, and in a few minutes the kettle was splattering steam and water over the stove. He placed two mugs on the table and washed out the stale tea leaves in the bottom of the teapot. From a small cupboard near the table he took down a glass gallon jar and reached inside, pulling out a handful of loose tea leaves and dropping them into the teapot. He then splashed some scalding water over the leaves.

As the brew was steeping, he said, "I think the weather is going to clear around midnight, Doctor. The wind is going to come around from the nor'west."

Grenfell looked at his pocket watch: 9:30 P.M. The wind was not as strong now. The two men sat down with their tea, and the skipper put a large molasses cake and a knife on the table almost as an afterthought. The doctor took the knife and cut off a slice. He was surprised to find he was ravenous.

After polishing off a large slice of the delicious cake, the doctor brushed crumbs from his clothes and crossed his legs. "I suppose you wouldn't mind if I ask you a few questions, Captain?" he said.

"No, Doctor, I wouldn't."

"How old are you?"

"I'm fifty-three, Doctor."

Grenfell looked at the skipper's white hair and wrinkled face; he looked at least seventy. "How long have you been coming to the Labrador?"

He thought for a moment, then said, "Forty-three years. I first came when I was ten years old, with my father and uncles. It hasn't all been smooth sailing, Doctor, but this year has been the worst one yet."

"Who owns the schooner you have out in the harbour? Is it yours?"

"We own the schooner, all right, but if we don't have a good voyage the fish merchant who supplied us with our grub and fishing gear will take it from us. This is why we stayed down here as long as we have. We should have been back by now. Excuse me for a moment, Doctor. I'd like to check on the weather."

Skipper Joe went outside to have a look around, and when he came back he said, "It's clearing away and the wind is dropping. If the wind goes nor'west it'll knock down the sea, and by daylight it should be pretty good. Maybe the boys will be able to get back then."

They sat in the kitchen, eating and drinking, when they heard a noise from inside the back room. The skipper jumped. "It's Molly, Doctor. She's awake."

Dr. Grenfell grabbed the lantern and went to her bedside. "How are you doing, my dear?" he asked.

Molly groaned. The skipper came in and grasped her hand. "Molly, you're going to be okay now. The doctor is here with you; you're going to be all right."

Molly shut her eyes and fell into a deep sleep. The white-haired skipper laid her hand down by her side.

It was now eleven o'clock.

The trap skiff was partly protected from the high swells rolling in. The six men had been listening to the horn on what they thought was their schooner, being blown by their father, and it was very comforting. Someone was out there and was concerned about them.

Bill was alert, always looking for any sign that could indicate a change in the weather. "Men, I think the snow is starting to clear up. The wind's shifted to the nor'west. The boat is starting to swing around."

"I'm willing to bet that in an hour from now we'll be able to see where we are," said Jack.

"It won't be too dark tonight because the skim of snow on the ground will make it a bit light," Bill said. "If we're able to see a landmark we recognize, we'll be able to get into the harbour."

The others agreed, but Bill cautioned them. "Don't get your hopes up too high, boys. You're not alongside Signal Hill now." No one spoke, knowing that they would still need a miracle to outlast the raging sea.

Gid broke the spell of silence that followed.

"I can see land in there, boys!"

"Where, Gid, where?" said Jack.

"In there," Gid screamed above the noise of the sea.

In a break through a snow squall, they all saw it.

"You're right, Gid!" Bill grinned. "It's the hill near the cabin."

Now there was a glimmer of hope. They all wanted to start rowing the boat toward the headland, but Bill knew it wouldn't be wise; no one knew for sure where the harbour entrance was. When it came on daylight, though, and if they were still afloat, they would have a chance.

FIFTEEN

The two men sat near the cabin's table. Before midnight, Dr. Grenfell observed that Molly had taken a turn for the worse, but he didn't mention it to the skipper.

Skipper Joe was sick with worry. Every few minutes he went to the window and looked out, before going outside to listen for sounds of his crew approaching. The weather had begun to clear, and now as he went outside, the snow and the wind from the northeast had stopped. He listened but heard only the roar of the sea.

The old man thought he might go up on the hill behind the cabin for a look, but he feared Molly was fading fast. He decided against it, in case she should stir and ask for him. When he went back into the cabin again, the doctor called to him from inside Molly's room.

"Captain, you had better come in here."

Skipper Joe went to the bedside. One look told him that the end had come.

My God. Is it possible that Molly is going to die? How will we ever live with that?

Molly opened her eyes and said her last words.

"Remember me, Jack."

Her breathing ceased, and she closed her blue eyes in death.

"She's gone, Captain." said Dr. Grenfell. "Molly is gone."

Later, Grenfell would write in his notes, "Around midnight she passed away."

Skipper Joe started sobbing. As the tears ran down his face, the young English doctor put his arm across the old man's shoulders to comfort him. Dr. Grenfell could feel the bony frame that supported the worry and sorrow contained within this broken man. It was amazing how tears could come from such a weather-etched face of steel, and yet they came from the man's heart, tears for the loss of Molly and the worry for his missing crew. What a mixture of sorrow!

"Don't worry, sir. I believe that she has gone to a better world. She doesn't have any pain now, so please get hold of yourself."

The skipper trembled as he walked out of the bedroom. "Oh, my, will it ever end?"

Grenfell pulled the white sheet up over Molly's small frame and offered a silent prayer. If only Skipper Joe's men had found him earlier, this might have ended differently, but now Molly was gone forever. If he told the broken old man what had really caused the death of the young girl it would probably cause his death too, so the doctor decided to destroy the evidence.

He walked out to the kitchen and spoke to the skipper about burning the soiled linens from Molly's bed. Was there any oil or kerosene around that he could use to start a fire in this wet weather? It was the best thing to do, he explained, rather than have them strewn about. Grenfell gave him his lantern, and the skipper went down to the stage and came back with two gallons of kerosene in an open can. The doctor rolled up all of Molly's personal effects in the fly- and maggot-infested blankets, then bundled it all inside a clean white sheet.

"I have matches, Captain," he said as they went outside.

"We might as well go up there on the hill and light the

fire," said Skipper Joe.

As they trudged through the freshly fallen snow, Grenfell thought about the incident that had happened at Mugford Tickle earlier that summer. Pearl, the young girl who had gotten pregnant, had begged to die, and she had gotten her wish. And now it had happened again. Molly, only a girl herself, had hidden the fact of her pregnancy from the skipper and paid the ultimate price as a result. In both cases the young women chose death over the shame and scorn they were certain to receive upon returning home to their families.

I wonder if people will ever become educated to the fact that life is real and it must be cherished?

They walked up a hill about three hundred feet from the cabin. The wind was veering to the northwest and the stars were beginning to show. "We'll light the fire here, Doctor," said Skipper Joe.

Grenfell laid down the stinking bundle. "Okay, you can pour the oil over it now, Captain. I'll light the match."

The old man poured half of the oil over the soiled linen, and Grenfell lit a match and threw it on the pile. It caught immediately and flared into the night sky.

Bill and his crew watched the land and the huge breakers that rolled in. The sky was beginning to show through the clouds, and he saw that it was going to clear up. "I don't know if we should make a run for it or not, or if we should wait 'til daylight," he said.

He scanned the landscape with eyes as sharp as any eagle's. "I'm not sure if that's our hill near the cabin or not, but I think it's too dangerous to stay here much longer."

Everyone was alert and restless. Suddenly, Jack jumped to his feet and pointed. "Look! Up there, boys!" he shouted. Up the slope of the hill, high above them, about four hundred yards away, was a bonfire.

"'Tis the old man!" Roy exclaimed.

"It must be Father up there," Fred agreed.

"Yes, it's him!" the others cheered.

"Now we know where we are!" Bill said, pointing. "There's the run, over there. But we can't move yet; there's too much sea."

Jack was puzzled. "I wonder what made Father think of lighting a bonfire?"

Fred laughed. "It had to be an act of God, or something." The boys felt proud of their father, and their chests swelled with love and admiration for him.

"Let's all call out, everyone together. He might hear us," Jack suggested.

Gid joined in. "When I count to three, we'll all yell together, as loud as we can."

"We'll call three times," Bill said, grinning.

They all agreed and got ready to stretch their lungs. On the count of one, two, three, they all yelled together: "HELLO!"

Dr. Grenfell and the skipper stood facing the ocean, the flames crackling before them. "My blessed Lord!" Skipper Joe yelled above the noise of the sea. "Listen, Doctor. I heard something."

Grenfell marvelled at the old man's hearing.

Then he heard it too. *Hello.*

"Yes, I hear it!" Grenfell exclaimed.

They both heard a third "hello" clearly. The old man went wild and pranced around, and for a moment Dr. Grenfell thought he was going to run off the cliffs.

"'Tis the boys, Doctor! I heard the boys! There, out there!"

Skipper Joe cupped his hands around his mouth and let out a scream the likes of which the English doctor had never heard before.

"Keep the fire blazing," said Grenfell. "They must have seen the fire."

Skipper Joe's eyes glistened as he took more kerosene and threw it over Molly's bloody nightgown and the fetus that had caused her death. The fire jumped higher and burned brighter.

"'Tis the boys, Dr. Grenfell, and they're out there somewhere around the Clummick, maybe in the lun of the island. We must keep the blaze high."

"Do you have any more of that kerosene, Captain?"

"Yes, Doctor, I do."

"You'll have to go and get more of it before the fire goes down, because there's no wood or brush around here to keep it going."

"Okay," said Skipper Joe, and he ran like a cat for the stage, swinging the lantern as he went.

Bill decided it was time to move.

"Listen, boys. I think the wind is going to pick up, and we're going to have to go before it does."

To a man, they were willing to chance it.

"Now that we know exactly where we are, thanks to Father and his fire, we'll have to make a run for it. It'll be chance work getting into the harbour in this darkness, because I can guarantee the sea is breaking right across the mouth. But we have no choice but to go now."

Staring toward the bonfire, he continued. "If the wind picks up and blows as hard as I've seen it in the past, our boat will be like matchsticks inside of an hour, because we'll never be able to keep the boats off the rocks. Let's go."

Bill manned the sculling oar in the rear as the man in the head of the boat pulled up the grapnel. The others pulled hard on their oars, and the trap skiff and the dories in tow started to make its way toward the small harbour. It was a rough ride for the little armada as it nosed its way through the boiling undertow close to the land, but in half an hour the crew had reached the harbour entrance.

It was a mass of whitecaps, as if the waves were breaking on shallow rocks, and flumes of spray were going high into the cliffs. "Hold everything now, boys," Bill instructed. "After the three seas roll in, we'll have to make a run for it. Hit or miss, it makes no difference."

If anyone could take them through, it was Bill. Each man was silent, concentrating on the danger ahead.

"Row!"

Fate was on their side, and the sea would have to go hungry for another while. They came through the harbour entrance without a hitch.

Fred smiled. "Thank God. We're safe."

SIXTEEN

Earlier in the night, after he had cleaned Molly and put her back in bed, Dr. Grenfell asked Skipper Joe if she had been courting any of the men. He wanted to find out as much as possible without having to tell the old man the real cause of her death. He had to step lightly, because he knew that the old man wasn't stupid. He would likely catch on if the doctor let something slip.

"My son, Jack, he is Molly's age and has been hanging around her. I don't know if he had anything to do with her, though. You know what I mean."

"I see. So what you're saying, Captain, is that Molly and Jack have been courting one another."

"Yes," replied the skipper. "Why?" Thoughts raced through his head. *Is there something that I don't know? What was Molly saying in her sleep—a baby?*

Grenfell was determined to keep his promise to Molly. Skipper Joe was about to ask him a question when the doctor cut him off.

"Your son Jack hasn't been sick, has he?"

"No."

"I didn't know. I'm asking because typhoid fever is very contagious, you know."

"I kept the men away from the shack. They've been staying aboard the schooner ever since Molly took sick."

"You did the right thing, sir."

The old man didn't respond, but Grenfell now knew who had gotten Molly pregnant. He knew he'd have to comfort Jack more than the others.

Despite the heartbreak of Molly's death, the old, weather-beaten skipper lived a happy moment when he saw the trap skiff enter the harbour mouth. At first he couldn't see if all the men were aboard. He ran down to the stage and waited, leaving Dr. Grenfell on the hillside.

Bill had the men row the boat directly to the stagehead, and as they approached, they examined the strange schooner.

"Look," Bill said, pointing to the *Albert*. She was anchored close to their own schooner. "That must be the vessel that was blowing the horn."

They saw men on deck in the light of the lanterns that hung in the rigging. Bill waved as they rowed along by them and they waved back.

Before they got close to the wharf they heard their father calling. "Is everyone on board, Bill?"

"Yes we're all here, Father."

"Well, thank God."

When they tied the boat on, the six men clambered up out of the boat and onto the wharf. They could hardly stand. The skipper went directly to Jack and put his arms around him and started crying, letting it all out.

"It's all right, Father, we're all here, safe and sound," Jack said, but the old man kept his arms around him and continued crying.

Fred stepped forward and put his arms around Jack and his father. "Father, try to get hold of yourself. Tonight our prayers have been answered."

The old man settled down and stopped crying. He told them all to come near him and listen.

"Boys, I have some sad news to tell you. Molly is dead. She passed away tonight around twelve o'clock."

A shocked silence followed. Jack broke into tears, and for a moment the men didn't know what was going to happen to him as he started shaking and fell to the ground. His grief was more than one could imagine. At just eighteen years of age, here he was, standing on a wharf at three in the morning, surviving an ordeal that very few men have in a full lifetime, and now he is told that the girl he loves, his first love, has died. And with her, a secret that should have been a source of joy. Only the toughest of people can cope with such tragedy.

It took some time for the men and Skipper Joe to settle him down. As they stood there and looked toward the brightly lit cabin, a figure appeared and stood in the doorway.

"Who is at the cabin, Father?" asked Bill, choking with grief.

"It's Dr. Grenfell. The storm drove him in here, but it was too late when he came. Molly was dying, and it was too late to save her."

They entered the warm cabin, where Grenfell's bright lantern gave the place an eerie, unsettling glow of sorrow and death that mingled with their gloomy thoughts. The place was foreign to them; they hadn't been there in such a long time. The crew were surprised to see how young the doctor was; he couldn't have been much older than a teenager.

"I'm Dr. Grenfell." He held out his hand to each of them as the skipper introduced his crew, leaving Jack last. Grenfell observed that the men looked much older than they really were.

Jack was so grief-stricken he could hardly say hello. Grenfell dared not tell him that Molly's last words were for him—it would only tear at his heart more. He would need close counselling.

The men sat around the table and looked at Dr. Grenfell. "You fellows were lucky that you didn't catch that awful disease," he said. "Your father did the right thing by having you stay on board the schooner."

Jack wasn't fooled. He was sure the doctor knew the real cause of Molly's death and was holding back. Physically and emotionally exhausted, he rested his head on his arm.

Skipper Joe was busy preparing the men a lunch, the soup that he had cooked the previous day. The men shrugged off their wet clothes and hung them up around the cabin, making an effort to avoid Molly's room. How would they ever be able to look at her, even if they wanted to? She had turned dark so quickly that Dr. Grenfell had wrapped her up and warned them against getting too close.

After the crew ate their meal they went out to the schooner, but before leaving, Skipper Joe said, "Listen, boys. Tomorrow we'll get ready to go back home. The fishing is over for the year."

Bill spoke for everyone. "Yes, Father, you're right. I made up my mind out there near that island tonight, and if I could have known my future before I left home, I wouldn't have even come down here at all this year."

Grenfell and Skipper Joe sat at the table. "We've seen great sorrow and great happiness in the space of these past few hours," the doctor said. "We'll never know the meaning of it all, Captain. Only the Great Maker knows what the end will be for every one of us."

Skipper Joe hung his head, listening to the young doctor's rich English accent.

"Have you thought about what really happened tonight, Captain?" It was a statement more than a question. "As we sit here near Molly's earthly remains, I suppose we are reminded that for every bad thing that happens, something good may come out of it."

"Yes," said the skipper, "I know what you mean. I've been thinking about it."

Dr. Grenfell said, "Do you realize that if Molly hadn't taken sick as she did and died, we would never have lit a fire, and your crew might have been lost?"

"Yes, Doctor, I have been thinking about that. It took the very thing that killed Molly to save the lives of my sons and my sharemen. May God forgive us all."

Dr Grenfell picked up a folder from the table. He looked over at Skipper Joe Budden and saw that the old man was finally giving in to sleep. The young doctor sighed and wrote five words across the file folder: THE CAPTAIN AND THE GIRL.

EPILOGUE

There are many stories told by Dr. Grenfell in his books and unpublished documents. He also related them in his lectures around the world. Reading his material, one can feel his despair, even though the incidents happened more than a hundred years ago.

There is one particular story that shows the primitive conditions Dr. Grenfell encountered. This may not be the actual word-for-word account taken from his writings and lectures, however it's as close as it can get to the actual event described in his notes from the fall of 1895.

Dr. Grenfell had been on the Labrador, way up north, working among the Inuit. He had stayed too long and came close to getting caught in the ice. It was now beginning to freeze over, and snow was beginning to cover the ground. To leave the small village of Hebron, the site of a Moravian Mission, the little vessel *Albert* had to break the ice to get out of the harbour. Once out into the mighty Labrador Sea it was all open water, and as they sailed along under full canvas for about fifty miles, the doctor and Captain Trezise began to reminisce about a man whom they had visited this time a year ago, and they wondered if he had made it through the winter. They decided to touch into the small cove where a mercantile business operated during the summer. They wanted to see if he was still around and inquire if he needed medical attention.

The little outpost in question wasn't a settlement or a village, as such. It was a group of four buildings with a wharf built to accommodate only small vessels such as the *Albert*. It wasn't a harbour either, just a shore sheltered by a group of islands that absorbed most of the impact from the large swells that rolled in. The outpost itself was on a barren island and was used during the summer season by fishermen who came from the south and needed supplies while fishing from the land. When the merchant closed up shop around October and went back to St. John's, he would get a reliable person to stay as caretaker. The merchant would supply the person with enough rough grub for the winter and some firewood—this depended on the length of the winter, of course—and in turn, the caretaker repaired and protected the owner's property.

On this bitterly cold morning in mid-December, Captain Trezise manoeuvred the *Albert*, with streaks of ice frozen to its sides, through the nest of shoals and small islands, to the wharf of this little outpost. As they neared the shore, they were surprised to see two men walking out to catch their lines. They were poorly clad, wearing only homemade clothing, from their sealskin boots to the caps on their heads.

Grenfell stepped ashore on the wharf and shook hands with them. He told them who he was, what he was doing and where he was headed. He was disappointed when the man he had visited there the previous year wasn't among them.

"I suppose you two men are the caretakers," Grenfell said in a kind of see-you-later tone of voice, eager to move on now that his contact wasn't present.

"Yes, Doctor," said one of the men, "we are the caretakers, but we've got our crowd with us, too."

Grenfell gave them a surprised look. "You men have your family with you? Women and children?"

"Yes," the man replied.

"So, the merchant is letting you live in his house for the winter. How nice of him."

"Oh, no, Doctor, we have our own house. Look, see," said the man, pointing to a small, barren hill a short distance away. It took a few seconds for the doctor and Captain Trezise to register smoke rising from a stovepipe.

"Oh, yes, I see it," said Grenfell, staring in the direction of the smoke.

"We built it ourselves in two days."

Grenfell thought about the women and children there. "Captain, can you spare enough time for me to hold a medical clinic here? It shouldn't take me more than an hour."

"Yes, Doctor, go ahead," said Captain Trezise. "We'll wait."

Grenfell grabbed his medical bag and went with the two men, and they walked ankle-deep in snow to the mud-covered hut protruding from the side of the hill. While they walked, the doctor asked, "Where is the man who was here last year, gentlemen?"

One of the men said, "Oh, he died late last winter or early spring, Doctor. He starved to death. He even ate his dog, trying to stay alive, you know."

They came to the hut, but Grenfell, dumbfounded, asked, "What did you say?"

No one replied, and the silence was broken when several dogs nearby started barking. To Grenfell's surprise, it sounded like they were inside the sod hut. He could smell the stench of them, and he balked at the vicious growling and barking coming from inside the dwelling.

"Good God, man," he whispered. "What do you have in there?"

"Don't worry about them, Doctor. They're our dogs. They won't hurt you, they're all penned up."

The man who appeared to be in charge stepped forward, opened the door and walked inside. In moments, he silenced the canines. "Come on in, Doctor, but watch your head; the door is low."

Grenfell hesitated for a moment before stepping inside. He said later that in the semi-darkness of the outer porch of this hut the only thing he could see through the seams in the boards on either side was the snarling teeth of hungry husky dogs. There were eight in all, penned up on either side of the porch.

The doctor braced himself, because he knew it wouldn't be very pleasant inside this dwelling. As he stepped into the inner room, there was a silence, as if there were no one present. The only light in this dwelling came from the ceiling, through a window in the roof, streaks of daylight made visible by the smoke in the air. A low partition divided the bunk area from the sitting room/kitchen, and the total length of the house was twenty feet by ten feet wide, including the filthy pens in the porch.

In the sitting room area of the house was an old, dilapidated homemade stove that smoked terribly. In the tiny kitchen, Grenfell spied two women sitting quietly on benches along the wall. They both stood up as the doctor entered, and before they were introduced, the women were bowing their heads to him. They were both heavy with child, and each wore sealskin boots and long black dresses that hung to the floor.

"This is a doctor—Dr. Grenfell—the one that we've heard about," said the lead man.

"Good day, ladies," Grenfell said in a very friendly voice. "And how are you today?" His confident, rich English accent was a balm to the ears, making people who were around him feel at ease.

"Fine, sir. Can we get you a cup of tea, Doctor?"

"Yes, please, ladies, but you'll have to make it quick, because we are moving south, hopefully ahead of the freeze-up."

Dr. Grenfell always made sure that he accepted people's hospitality, no matter how humble it was; he said that it made him part of them.

"We heard that you were a doctor down north, and good news like that gets around," said one of the women.

"Yes, I've been on the coast since July. We never thought there were women and children living at this station. Do you mind if I ask you some questions about your pregnancies and have a look at your youngsters? I know that you have children here, because I saw their tracks in the snow."

"We have four children each. The oldest is seven and the youngest is one."

Grenfell found this hard to believe. "You have eight children here now?"

"Yes, we do, Doctor, and all in perfect health."

"Do your children have any problems with minor sickness, such as toothache, earache, or dysentery?"

One of the women spoke up. "Yes, the youngsters have the earache often, but the men take care of that."

"What do the men do to ease earaches?"

"They usually blow baccy smoke in their ears, that is, when they have any baccy."

The doctor rolled his eyes. "Where are the children now?"

"They're all in the other room," the woman replied.

"May I see them?"

"Yes, Doctor." With this, the two women went into the room and brought the children out.

Grenfell was amazed at how well they looked. They were thin, but otherwise healthy and strong. "They are fine-looking children, ladies," he said. The children were extremely quiet—none of them spoke out of shyness. The two youngest were in their mothers' arms.

After the doctor examined them, the women sent them back into the room. When all was quiet, Grenfell asked them, "When do you expect your babies to arrive?"

One of them said that she was expecting in March, and the other said that her baby would be due in February. "Who will help you at the birth?" Grenfell asked.

"We'll help each other. This is how we've had all our

youngsters." The doctor didn't say anything more. He was almost afraid to ask any more questions, afraid of what he might find.

Grenfell took out his notebook and wrote: "...this dwelling is approx 10 feet by 20 feet and has eight children and four adults; this includes two men and two expectant mothers. Two people had been living with them for awhile, but have now gone up into the bay; this makes fourteen people living here, and eight dirty, half-starved husky dogs penned up in the porch..."

It was unbelievable!

After he walked outside the dwelling and had taken in a few breaths of fresh air, Dr. Grenfell again probed the men for details concerning the caretaker who had been there a year ago. They told him they had known the man quite well because "he was our mother's brother," and there was no doubting fate: in late April or early May he had starved to death after he had eaten everything he had, including his pet dog.

They called him aside. "Come here. We'll show you something, Doctor."

Grenfell walked with the men for fifty yards. "Look," one pointed. "There it is. My brother and I put up this cross for Uncle Ike and his dog."

The grave was covered with snow and the cross was clearly visible. It read: TO UNCLE IKE AND SWATCH.

One of the men turned to face Grenfell. "In the spring, when the fish merchant came, he went into the shack where Uncle Ike used to live, and over on the wooden bunk he found his remains wrapped in an old blanket. Well, the merchant wouldn't touch him. He sent word to us up in the bay to come out, because we were the ones who were related to him. We came out, and sure enough, he was dead. We also found something else. Near his bunk was a small wooden box, and in it we found the remains of his dog. There wasn't a peck of meat on the bones. The brain was scooped out, and even the teeth were picked clean. We then took all of the bones of the dog and put them inside his coat, next to his skeleton—all that was left of Uncle Ike—and buried them, wrapped in old brin bags that the fish merchant gave us. May God rest his poor soul."

Grenfell was very shaken. He said a silent prayer and made ready to leave for the schooner. "I'll give you the medicine that the women need," he said, "and these are eardrops and toothache drops for the children. I told the women how to use it. Wait here for a moment."

The young doctor went aboard the *Albert*, and in a few minutes he came back with a wooden box. "I have a few things here for the children: a few candies and a few toys. Men, look after your women and children, please."

As they shook hands, the men gave him assurances that they would do their best for their wives. Grenfell waved to the women and children, who were now assembled in front of the sod hut. They waved back.

As they sailed away, Dr. Grenfell said, "I can't see how they will ever live to see spring. May God protect them." In a few minutes, they were out of sight and gone.

The following summer, Dr. Grenfell was again on the Labrador coast with his medical mission and steamed along by the same little outpost, anxious to inquire about the two families he'd left there in the fall. He decided to touch in, and after the vessel was tied up he went ashore for a walk. In the distance he could see the sod hut, but this time it was beginning to turn green with grass and shrubs. He walked up to the door, and all was silent. It was obvious that there was no one inside, but he could still smell the stench of the dogs from the past winter.

With nobody home to talk to, he decided to visit the grave of the starved man and his dog, Uncle Ike and Swatch, and upon getting there, he saw another cross that was newly erected.

"I wonder who that is," he mused, and as he bent low to

take a closer look, he read, written in crude crayon letters:
IN LOVING MEMORY OF MAGGIE AGE 36 YEARS AND HER BELOVED
DAUGHTER WHO BOTH DIED FEB 20, GONE TO THEIR REST.

This was the older of the two women. She had died in
childbirth.

Grenfell broke down and wept.

Afterword

But there is more to this story than Grenfell knew.

On the day following the storm, the *Albert* left before dawn and Skipper Joe gave the order to get ready to leave the Labrador. He took boards from the cabin walls and made a coffin for Molly, stowing her remains below deck. They were home at Seldom-Come-By in three days, entering the harbour with their flags flying at half-mast.

Molly's family and the whole community were devastated as she lay waking in her home for two days. "Amazing Grace" was sung once again, not by the young maiden this time, but for her.

Heartbroken, Jack left his home of Seldom-Come-By and settled at Greenspond, Bonavista Bay. There he fell in love with and married a young girl by the name of Mary Pond. After several years working in a liver factory at Greenspond, he moved back home to Seldom-Come-By and began going to the Labrador once again. In 1897, Jack and Mary had a son whom they named Joe, after his grandfather, Skipper Joe Budden.

In researching this story, I contacted Mr. Les Budden of Labrador City, formerly of Seldom-Come-By. He informed me that he had an uncle Jack Budden of Seldom-Come-By who went to the Labrador in a fishing schooner in 1905, fishing for cod. Les Budden said that "I heard my father say many times that while Great-uncle Jack was down there that year, he caught the dreaded disease typhoid fever and died. His older brothers made a coffin for him and salted him away until they returned in the fall."

After Jack was buried, his wife took young Joe and went back to her family at Greenspond. Young Joe grew up fast, and at an early age he joined the famous sealing fleet and sailed on the *Stephano* with the world's greatest sealing captain, Abram Kean.

"I was standing only a few feet away from Old Abram Kean when he ordered the *Newfoundland's* crew off his ship," he said. "Some of them were cold, wet, and crying, and told him they weren't going to make it to their ship, but he drove them off anyway."

Within days, seventy-eight of these sealers lost their lives due to a vicious snowstorm. Young Joe carried the newspaper with the story for the rest of his life and told the story to anyone who lent an ear.

After a career of travelling the world on ships, he retired to the lumber town of Roddickton and became a lumberjack. Joe passed away at his home in Roddickton in 1985, at the age of eighty-eight.

Earl B. Pilgrim

- About the Author -

Earl Baxter Pilgrim was born in St. Anthony, Newfoundland in 1939, son of Norman and Winnie (Roberts) Pilgrim. He received his early education in Roddickton, Newfoundland, later studying Forestry at the College of Trades and Technology in St. John's.

He began his adult career in 1960 as an infantryman in the Canadian Army, serving with the Princess Patricia's Canadian Light Infantry. While there, he became involved in the sport of boxing, eventually becoming the Canadian Light Heavyweight Boxing Champion.

Following a stint in the Forces, Pilgrim took a job as a forest ranger with the Newfoundland and Labrador Forestry Department. During this time, he came to recognize the plight of the big game population on Newfoundland's Great Northern Peninsula. After nine years as a forest warden, he became a wildlife protection officer with the Newfoundland Wildlife Service.

For seventeen years, he has devoted his efforts to the growth and conservation of the big game population on the

Great Northern Peninsula. Under his surveillance, the moose and caribou populations have grown and prospered at an astonishing rate. As a game warden and a local storyteller, he has gained the respect of conservationist and poacher alike.

Earl Pilgrim has been presented with a number of awards: the Safari International, presented by the Provincial Wildlife Division; the Gunther Behr, presented by the Newfoundland and Labrador Wildlife Federation; and the Achievement "Beyond the Call of Duty" Award, presented by the White Bay Central Development Association.

Among his many achievements are contributions as a conservationist for waterfowl. He has made a hobby of raising eider ducks, and it has been estimated that eighty percent of all nesting eiders in Newfoundland developed from his original twelve ducks.

He is married to the former Beatrice Compton of Englee. They have four children and make their home in Roddickton, Newfoundland.

The Captain and the Girl is Earl B. Pilgrim's fifth book. All of his previous books are Canadian Best-sellers.

...also by Earl B. Pilgrim...

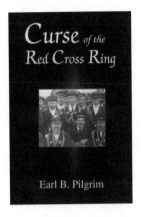

"...Pilgrim's fourth tour de force..."
- Atlantic Books Today

Earl B. Pilgrim has masterfully constructed a story of murder, betrayal, and ultimate heroism. *Curse of the Red Cross Ring* follows the trail of Sod Mugford: fisherman, lumberjack, murderer. It is based on the true happenings of 1928 and 1929, when he killed an innocent schoolteacher and fled north to the small town of L'Anse au Pigeon, Newfoundland. There he thought he would be safe from the law, but what he hadn't counted on was one man to whom the townspeople entrusted their lives in times of trouble. That man was Azariah Roberts.

ISBN 1-894463-11-0. 334 pages. $19.95

Flanker Press Ltd.
P O Box 2522, Stn C, St. John's
Newfoundland, Canada, A1C 6K1

Toll Free: 1-866-739-4420   E-mail: info@flankerpress.com

...also by Earl B. Pilgrim...

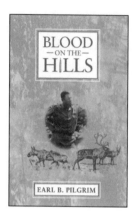

"...a master storyteller..."
- sieved.com

Wildlife officer Earl Pilgrim is on a mission. The moose and caribou populations on the Great Northern Peninsula have been decimated, and he has promised the government of Newfoundland and Labrador to end the poaching threat. Through the character John Christian, Pilgrim takes the reader into his world of stakeouts, bare-knuckled standoffs, and high-speed chases across the frozen barrens of the north. *Blood on the Hills* is an autobiography. It is a tale of selfless determination involving great personal risk to carry out a mission that seemed impossible.

ISBN 1-894463-07-2. 143 pages. $14.95

Flanker Press Ltd.
P O Box 2522, Stn C, St. John's
Newfoundland, Canada, A1C 6K1

Toll Free: 1-866-739-4420   E-mail: info@flankerpress.com

...also by Earl B. Pilgrim...

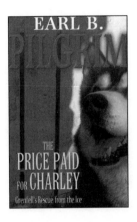

"...discloses a very human Grenfell..."
- Grenfell Historical Society

The great northern Newfoundland doctor Sir Wilfred T. Grenfell once said "Real joy comes not from ease or riches or from the praise of men but from doing something worthwhile." *The Price Paid for Charley* is Earl Pilgrim's tribute to the doctor from England who changed so many lives in Newfoundland and Labrador. It describes Dr. Grenfell's brave attempt at battling the elements to reach one of his patients, Charley Hancock, and the shortcut that nearly cost him his life.

ISBN 1-894463-05-6. 207 pages. $14.95

Flanker Press Ltd.
P O Box 2522, Stn C, St. John's
Newfoundland, Canada, A1C 6K1

Toll Free: 1-866-739-4420   E-mail: info@flankerpress.com

...also by Earl B. Pilgrim...

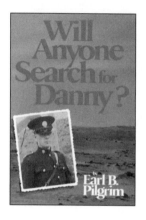

"...gripping, inspirational..."
- Ted Williams

This story has been written as a memorial to the search party from Englee, Newfoundland who went far beyond the call of duty to search for the lost ranger, Danny Corcoran, fighting all the elements that Nature could unleash. *Will Anyone Search for Danny?* is the heartbreaking true story of the townspeople who came to love this young man and pulled together to help him when he needed them most.

ISBN 1-894463-01-3. 270 pages. $16.95

Flanker Press Ltd.
P O Box 2522, Stn C, St. John's
Newfoundland, Canada, A1C 6K1

Toll Free: 1-866-739-4420   E-mail: info@flankerpress.com

More Praise for Earl B. Pilgrim

"[Earl Pilgrim] has received several awards for his work in conservation, including the Gunther Behr Award, presented in 1984 by the Newfoundland and Labrador Wildlife Federation. Encouraged by J. R. Smallwood, in 1986 Pilgrim turned his storytelling abilities into a book, *Will Anyone Search for Danny?*, followed in 1989 by *The Price Paid for Charley.*" – *Encyclopedia of Newfoundland and Labrador*

"I have great respect for Mr. Pilgrim and his passion for big game on the Great Northern Peninsula. His efforts to preserve the moose and caribou populations have been as successful as his writing endeavours, both of which have earned him prestigious awards." – Hon. Charles J. Furey, Minister of Tourism, Culture and Recreation, Government of Newfoundland and Labrador.

WILL ANYONE SEARCH FOR DANNY?

"This is the gripping, inspirational story of a legendary game warden written by another legendary game warden—Earl Pilgrim, one of Canada's most successful boxers, an indefatigable crusader for the restoration of moose and caribou and a Master Raconteur. It is a proper tribute to both men and the wild, harsh, lovely land they have guarded so well." – Ted Williams, Contributing Editor of *Audobon Magazine* and *Gray's Sporting Journal*

"The descriptions of the search activities in *Will Anyone Search for Danny?* are strikingly familiar even though they occurred more than 60 years ago. I recommend this book be in the library of every search and rescue professional, career or volunteer." – Chris Long, *SAR*SCENE

THE PRICE PAID FOR CHARLEY

"This book sees Sir Wilfred Grenfell through the eyes of the local people. It depicts Grenfell the way he was seen and the esteem in which he was held. He was respected for his scientific and medical knowledge and ability—almost seen as a superhuman, and yet he was also seen by the people as a frail human who could not really cope with the elements of a northern culture as well as the local people." – Hon. Chris Decker, Minister of Health, Government of Newfoundland and Labrador

"*The Price Paid for Charley* records historical facts generally unknown about Grenfell's famous "Ice Pan Adventure." Mr. Pilgrim's research discloses a very human Grenfell and the sometimes desperate people that he served, making this a very readable and thrilling adventure." – John McGonigle, Sir Wilfred Thomason Grenfell Historical Society

BLOOD ON THE HILLS

"There is no doubting [Earl Pilgrim] is a master storyteller." – *sieved.com*

"This is an excellent book about the necessity of protection of wildlife in rural Newfoundland. Very well written, it tells, sometimes in graphic detail, the results of indiscriminate slaughter of moose and caribou in closed season." – Mike McCarthy, *The Telegram*

"*Blood on the Hills* is a great read for anyone interested in wildlife enforcement issues, particularly poaching, and how community residents can help fight it." – Bill Power, Outdoors Columnist, *The Telegram*

"In *Blood on the Hills* the author uses his expert storytelling abilities to preserve some of the memories he's collected during his years working as a wildlife officer." – *The Newfoundland Herald*

CURSE OF THE RED CROSS RING

"The greatest Newfoundland story ever told." – *The Downhomer*

"Pilgrim's fourth tour de force...gives the reader an idea of how isolated communities that have no police force attempt to maintain law and order, not always successfully, and sometimes with tragic results." – *Atlantic Books Today*

"Pilgrim weaves [a] fascinating tale...sharply visual and amazing. It's extremely readable, because what he has is a voice, knowledgeable and authentic." – *The Telegram*

"*Curse of the Red Cross Ring* is full of mystery, murder and twisting plots." – *The Nor'wester*

"A job well done." – *The Northern Pen*